Thruplicity
Part two:
Kissing Cousins

D. Edward Delmar

Book and logo design: D. Edward Delmar
Cover art adapted from stock by Felix Dion
ISBN: 978-1-7324648-5-8
eBook ISBN: 978-1-7324648-4-1

DEDICATION

To Goldilocks and friends.

D. Edward Delmar

ACKNOWLEDGMENTS

Without the help of a few husbands and wives and some stray boyfriends, none of this would have been possible.

Some men think with their dicks, others with their hearts. Here are a few whose dicks have tremendous imaginations and hearts.

D. Edward Delmar

PROLOGUE

NOTICE OF CEASE AND DESIST

Richard [redacted] and Seth [redacted]
[address redacted]

Dear Daniel [redacted],

This letter has been served as notice of your unwarranted harassment activities, or the equivalent thereof, that has been on-going in recent weeks. **Therefore, you are required to cease and desist all verbal and physical attacks, including, but not limited to: improper use and distribution of likenesses in the form of photos and video material circulated through the internet.**

If you do not cease all related acts a harassment lawsuit will be commenced against you.

The previously conducted actions are unwanted, unwelcome, and have become unbearable. Due to the aforementioned harm you have caused, this cease and desist shall serve as a pre-suit letter demanding that you provide us written assurance that you will refrain from further actions that could be deemed as harassment.

If you do not comply with this cease and desist letter within the aforementioned time-period, then a lawsuit may be filed in the proper jurisdiction seeking monetary damages as well as pursuing all available legal remedies for your harassment.

Sincerely,
[redacted]
Attorney at Law

* * *

Voicemail

Daniel
Mobile

Transcription Beta (low confidence)
"Hey it's Daniel just calling to let you know that um I've moved now but I'm broke so if you need to find me I'm at _____ street by the _____ bodega look for the crack wars and ugly shuts I'm next door if you need to fine me not that you will um hey I know you hate me and um I guess I'm on Richard's ship list and he blocked my number and OK I got it but it's kind of you know kind of skippy thing to do even if I know I know blah blah blah but um um you can call me if you have time because give a guy a second chance right I have been drinking because it's just me with the bottle now baby OK I'm off to wander in the woods…"

Was this transcription useful or not useful

* * *

Voicemail

Daniel
Mobile

Transcription Beta (low confidence)

"A restraining order a restraining order jesus you two are a piece of worth I cannot believe you duckers you lousy pieces of ship _____ believe you would do this like you don't even trust me duck you duckers…"

Was this transcription useful or not useful

* * *
Voicemail

Unknown caller
Mobile

Transcription Beta (low confidence)

"Oh Seth you've been a naughty naughty boy and you will be punished you and Daniel and Richard will have a lot to answer for and that day is coming soon _____ for now…"

Was this transcription useful or not useful

Book One:
The Third Dick

CHAPTER ONE: KYLE

Kyle felt his luck was changing. The first indication was the gorgeous man hovering over him and the sensation of his insides being massaged by a silken invasion. The second was the motherfucking view. Who else gets plowed in a virtual treehouse? Better than wanking in Mom's basement, that was for sure.

Since graduation, since his dickwad of a boyfriend dumped him for a grad student, he'd been holed up in a dingy downstairs room, stalking online career sites. For work (the only he could find in this fucking farm town) he'd hide in the back of Dunkin' Donuts praying no one he knew would see him. Humiliation had crawled up into his shirt and was peeking out from behind his collar. When he wasn't microwaving tasteless sandwiches and shoveling out 'wonder donuts,' he was hiding, sleeping, or refreshing his pictures on gay fuck-me apps.

He'd been stalking the married couple *"2-4ThePrice"* for months, just hoping they'd take pity on a well-educated (and endowed) 23-year old. Other than the fact that they were smoking hot with impressive equipment, they displayed a certain *je ne sais who knows what*. Their pictures looked like they came out of a Herb Ritts coffee table book. What he could see of the house resembled Frank Lloyd Wright on crack. And their interests: theatre, writing, gardening, art, movies, Becket, oral sex, frottage…who could ask for anything more?

It took quite a miracle and a prayer to get here. The gray-haired one, the guy who answered all the Scruff texts (the one who was fucking him upside down right now) said he was too young, that he had sweaters older than Kyle. But every time he looked at the gray-haired guy's picture he creamed. First off, he had looks you'd see in a high-class advertising firm like on TV, the kind of guy you'd think was a "cad" or a "roué" except for his sweet crooked smile and sad, wonky squint. Thick gray hair, tight Daddy abs, (no, no, he insisted, never Daddy), ripped *Uncle* abs, swimmer's chest, and his long, long…legs. Somewhere between 35 and 40 he'd guess. Richard, his name was (or "the smooth one."). Well, he was a goner, wanted that man inside him bad.

The other (Seth, the furry one) was the complete opposite: a silver back gorilla of a man: all curly hair, thatched chest and legs, and balls that could fill your mouth for days. Seth's abs were no less rippled, but he was thick and strong, low to the ground. He had a well-groomed beard, flecked with just enough gray, and one beguiling dimple peeking out on his cheek. His smile looked like an infection he wanted to catch: toothy (a slight split between his teeth like Madonna), and maybe just a little bit of trouble.

Kyle longed to be spit-roasted by these two, taking turns flipping from one to the next, with all of them exploring the necessary geography of their bodies.

The gray-haired one (*Richard, Richard, Richard*, he reminded himself, as if saying the name would conjure him up) was reticent; he felt awkward with such a young guy. Kyle countered by telling him his drama teacher popped his cherry at his own high school graduation party, in the same sad basement room he slept in now. Plus he'd fucked two of his college professors who were also married… to each other! He'd had group scenes in Florida, Washington, Cancun, and even Soho in London (the fragrance of warm beer mixed with poppers would forever remind him of a cockney lad with a huge uncircumcised dick and red pubic hair). So, he pleaded, he was experienced. They wouldn't be corrupting him any more than he had already corrupted himself.

Richard continued to demur (although he kept on responding to his texts!). Since the two only played together (it said right there in their Scruff profile), he figured all was lost. He kept them in the favorite category, checking out their pictures every chance he got (they never re-locked the private album). In addition to these two hot studs, there was another dick in one of the shots – an extra long. He didn't know who that one belonged to, or why it was there, but he enlarged the picture from time-to-time, just to study it.

Who was the third dick? Will I ever meet the third dick?

It came as a surprise when **2-4ThePrice** pinged him that morning. He was stuffing a batch of "hash browns" into the microwave when he heard that distinct "schwing" sound indicating someone on Scruff had texted him. Ducking behind a donut rack, he peeked into his phone and saw a note from **2-4**. Jesus fucking Christ, he hardened before he even clicked on it!

Please let's do tonight please let's do tonight, please let's do tonight.

Heart pounding, he fumbled with the phone, nearly dropping it into the crullers, but managed to grab it in time to glimpse the text: "plans tonight?"

He rushed to type the reply before the alarm for the hash browns dinged. "None. Unless I'm with you LOL."

And then he waited. And waited. He delivered the hash browns (*is there anything else I can get for you you have a nice day no we don't accept tips okay if you must*). He refrained from texting again, not wanting to sound (read?) over eager, for in the gay hookup world that was as bad as "needy" in the straight woman world.

Still nothing.

The day dragged on, relentlessly dull, his hope now shriveled to the size of a Munchkin. He was just about to punch out, just about to finish this hellish day, when one last drive-through customer appeared. He looked at the monitor to see a bright red convertible and a gray blob driving it.

Oh great, he thought. Another midlife crisis grabbing *a large decaf Iced Macchiotto with a squirt of Hazelnut and Mocha with Splenda for my diet and oh how about a vanilla cake batter donut because I've been a good boy.*

Why did I go to art school?

The voice that came back sounded young, energetic: "Large black iced tea, no lemon."

"Anything else?"

"No thank you, that will be it."

"Drive on up."

Kyle scooped out the ice, filled the cup, slapped on the lid. He was mentally pulling off his stupid apron, slipping out into the parking lot, racing home to wash the stench of donuts off of him, and veg in front of the TV and scroll through Scruff. Maybe fap away to today's near miss.

The red Porsche Spyder pulled up to the window; Kyle duly noted the lux car and sighed. He reached for the jumbo straw and said to the gleaming red hood of the car: "That'll be 2.65."

"Here," the man said, holding out his hand. "Keep the change."

Figuring it was three dollars, which would give him a whopping 35 cent tip, he reached for it, his other hand already untying the apron. When he grabbed a twenty, he felt stunned. He looked at the hand holding the bill, followed the long, toned arm to its owner: a handsome silver-haired guy, somewhere between 35 and fucking hot. Kyle stared at his dual reflections in the man's sunglasses as he reached out with the drink, napkin, and straw.

"Thank you." The man took a moment to situate his drink in the cup holder, tear off the straw wrapper with his teeth, punch it through the lid. That task neatly completed, he lowered his sunglasses, like Tom Cruise, but handsome, and said "What time do you get off?"

Kyle's dick responded before he could. Even though it took a moment for Kyle to recognize the face in front of him, his penis stood at full attention.

"Two-fer?" he asked, his voice faint. "I mean two-for-the-price?" How the fuck do you address a Scruff avatar come to life? "I'm sorry…" *Richard Richard Richard,* he scolded himself. Why was he apologizing? He straightened up, found his voice. "I get off right now." He yanked his apron off. "Whatcha got in mind?" God that was cool, even though his heart was beating like a tympani.

"Follow me."

"Now?" Kyle looked around. Had his manager heard him?

"Unless you've got someplace better to go."

"No!" He realized he was almost shouting when his manager, a nice gramma of a lady, turned in his direction. "No – I'm parked right behind in the lot."

The man placed his sunglasses back on his nose, smiled in a goofy crooked kind of way, and pulled out.

Kyle hollered goodbye, tore to his car, caught up with the red Spyder at the exit. He checked his teeth in the mirror, fished between his seat cushions for any lost mint, fussed with his hair, and followed the gleaming red sports car onto the main drag (which was, for this shitty town, hardly a drag, Dunkins seemed to be the highlight, that and an Exxon station with a Subway). He couldn't help but feel self-conscious in his dinged-up gray Toyota (which had been Mom's), and his polyester uniform pants and shirt. That car, for one thing, must have cost half a mil, easy. And where the hell was he following him? Was this some kind of ruse? Was he going to find himself trapped in some human centipede? (Not a bad idea if he was sewn mouth to ass between these two hot guys). He looked at his phone on the passenger seat and thought of reaching for it, texting his friend Harris to give him the GPS like when they warn you about these hookups. But something in his head (and his groin) said this guy was okay.

It wasn't until the Spyder pulled into a shrouded driveway that Kyle felt his first "holy fuck" moment. As the red car disappeared into the woods, he realized that he was going to "that house," the one his family had screeched about when it was being constructed. "That house" was the only modern glass masterpiece in a sea of split-level ranches and ancient colonials. "That house" was Kyle's personal holy grail, his Mecca, Emerald City. He'd watch it longingly from the back of the minivan when his parents drove him to soccer practice. Them bitching and moaning the whole time about the *effrontery* of bad taste. He longed to run up the hill when the leaves began to fall and the glimmering glass edifice gradually emerged from the hillside. The house was a mysterious monolith plopped down in the woods.

His parents had whispered, in tones none too subtle, about the "two guys" or "two fellas" who were building it. *They were from the city, don't you know. They might be hairdressers or something. You know how those types are. Not that there's anything wrong with that but in this small town do you think there's really a place for them here wouldn't they rather be in the city?*

Even as a budding sixteen year old he imagined the two men in that house, drinking champagne and running around naked. Once he got his driver's license, and the guys had moved in, he would slow down on his way past the house (in winter, when it was visible amidst the bare trees) trying to catch a glimpse of a naked guy somewhere in the windows.

Now he was driving up that driveway, snaking into the trees, behind a fucking Spyder! *2-4ThePrice* was delivering him from his humdrum life.

Or so he told himself.

Richard said that big furry Seth was out of town, and no, it didn't matter if they played, Seth was cool with it. *Would you like a cocktail sure why not?* And before he knew it his hand was down the guy's shirt, his tongue was being gently sucked out of his mouth, and his crotch was straining in his polyester pants.

Richard's skin felt like silk, his face smooth, slightly lined, and chiseled. His big brown eyes, which looked kind of sad in pictures, were quite merry. Yeah, that was the word, not like Christmas, but nice, kind, warm.

"I gotta take a shower," Kyle said, aware that Richard smelled like Dial soap and lemons and he smelled like donuts and grease.

"I know. You're not on my diet!" Richard burrowed his face beneath Kyle's arm and inhaled deeply.

Before he knew it, clothes were off, legs were up in the air and he was being plowed by an expert. He found himself somewhat distracted, not because of the man, who was one hot…*Uncle*…but because he had finally made it to this place, this hallowed moment. Now he was one of the naked guys he'd wished he'd seen all those years ago. He was in the window, he was folded over and…

"Where'd you go?" Richard asked, his eyes looking so deeply into Kyle's they almost hurt.

Kyle smiled, adoring the moment and this gentle, hot man sliding in and out with tenderness and strength. Rather than answer, he closed his eyes, shut out the gorgeous sights and just let himself feel, feel it all: the swirl of the tequila, the rippled muscles holding him, the unquenchable thirst to drink in this man, this fuck. He didn't answer, but he began to moan, at first just low in his throat; with each new thrust, he couldn't help but cry out a little bit more.

"Yeah," Richard said, coaxing each gasp with a sudden plunge or retreat.

Soon their voices were a chorus of moans and yeahs and Kyle knew he would blow and could he hold on just a bit more, could this feeling last before he exploded *and oh please let it last please let it*...

"What the fuck is going on?"

The voice came from above. His instincts made him jump, a deer in the woods. He rushed to remove himself from this act, feeling as if he had done wrong, been caught by a cop or something. But Richard continued fucking and he could feel the steady climb to the top. He was pinned, back against the floor, now it felt great and horrible and forbidden and he was caught *and this is what everyone warns you about*.

Now storming, pounding, the whole house shaking as someone thundered toward them like a charging buffalo.

"What. The. Fuck. Is. Going. On?"

The voice, loud, deep, sharp, was right above them.

Kyle opened his eyes to see the reddened face of the other guy. Seth! Nostrils flared, chest heaving. And look at that hair peeking out from his shirt *shut up oh shit oh shit oh shit he could fuck me too if he just oh Christ*...

It was too late, now he was going to cum and Richard's "yeahs" grew louder and together they were moaning and he was horrified and absolutely crashing over a tidal wave of orgasm and he couldn't help but sing out, a choir, fireworks, bang, explode! Seth collapsed on top of him, their bodies shuddering together in seismic spasms of ecstasy. Although humiliation lay just behind his orgasm, he couldn't help but gasp in delight as Richard gently pulled himself out.

Now Kyle looked up and his eyes met Seth's. He saw fury. Richard took his time, kissed him on the face, on the neck, on the chest as he gently rolled off and looked up.

"Seth," he said, casually, nothing out of the ordinary. "I thought you weren't going to be home until late."

Kyle couldn't grab his clothes fast enough, tripping over himself as he yanked them on and hopped up the stairs, out of the house, into his car, speeding down the driveway. Behind him he imagined explosions and turmoil. He looked at the house disappearing in his rearview mirror, half expecting to see a chair fly through one of the huge windows.

A half-mile down the road, heart bursting, he pulled over to catch his breath. His dick, still hard in his pants, discharged another load and he quivered with his second orgasm of the evening. He gulped to catch his breath, steady himself.

Fuck, he thought. *My life isn't changing after all. At least, not the way I want it.*

Voicemail

Unknown caller
Mobile

Transcription Beta (low confidence)

"Well well well Richard you've been up to no good I can see that now and soon everyone will mark my words I look forward to a lot of fun later bye I can tell you're pleased with yourself well we'll see what happens next..."

Was this transcription useful or not useful

* * *

Voicemail

Caller unknown
phone

Transcription Beta (low confidence)

"This is Sarah from _____ Services and we were given your name as a reference for Daniel _____ and were hoping for a call back you can reach me at 203-562-_____ or if you could leave a message and let me know a good time where I could reach you I'd appreciate it."

Was this transcription useful or not useful

CHAPTER TWO: DYLAN

Dylan is grateful for the towel rack, just the right height to hide behind when he steps out of his shorts. He's not ashamed of his dick or anything, far from it. He just likes to give his partners a chance to ease into him, to get used to the good stuff before they see the rumpled and reddened flesh on his legs.

"The air is great tonight. Crisp and cool." The voice is soft, throaty. The hunk (he forgets was his name Seth? Is that right?) nestles further down into the hot tub, leans back his head, closes his eyes, releasing a loud, satisfied sigh.

Dylan takes a moment to breathe in the evening air, the lingering scent of summer's last roses. He's happy for the dry, breezy night. Soon the leaves, gently flecked with gold, will be taking their kaleidoscopic ride through autumn. The sun, just squinting over the ridge, splaying through the trees, rakes across Dylan's tight, military-honed abs in dappled patches of amber light.

He looks down at his arm, at the Semper Fi tattoo. He just glimpses at the other one, below: "Blake." Goosebumps run up his arms, down his legs, halting at the thick keloided skin. He swings his arms back and forth, quick hugs to warm up, to flex his pecs.

"Hop in before you catch cold!" the hunk (Seth? Serge?) in the tub calls out. "It's goin' down to 50 tonight."

Now Dylan is aware of the big brown eyes caressing his torso and neck. Soon he'll have to emerge from behind the towels; soon he'll have to reveal his deformity, here in the midst of this splendor. He looks up at the glass structure, towering overhead, its square roof stretching above the trees. He hates the word awesome but feels true awe when he looks up.

Wind chimes tinkle from the pergola as the breeze whispers through the hickories. Dylan inhales again, deeply, emerges from behind the towels, slipping into the water without a splash.

Now those eyes are devouring him again, he can feel it. Turning toward the hunk, he smiles, hoping he isn't blushing. This isn't any life he is used to, not the saggy two-family house he'd grown up in outside Boston in Sommerville. Here, on this outdoor deck, surrounded by trees, crafted wood timbers stretching up toward the house, he can imagine himself in Hollywood or the Maine coast.

"It's a lot, but we call it home," the hunk says, just a taste of Brooklyn in the syllables. "Come here."

Now their eyes meet; Dylan feels himself pulled, as if by magnets, by underwater currents, by whirlpools that might drag him down. Strong hands grasp him by the biceps, legs wrap around his waist, and now his mouth is engulfed. Maybe they should just drown like this, like lovers in an opera, succumbing to the beauty of their tragic, yearning love, their consuming passions.

"Marble encased in satin," the hunk says, running his hands over Dylan's thick pecs, over the curve of his shoulders, down the arms again. "The marble faun."

Some things this guy says don't make sense, not exactly. But they sound poetic, deep beyond his experience. He blinks again and smiles.

Now the hunk is on top of him, like a kid on Santa's lap, and they twirl around the pool, from one side to the next. "The Ode to Billie Joe," an old song his mother loved, plays on the outdoor speakers, adding a touch of southern menace to the moment.

Hands grab him by his cheeks and he wants to be impaled face first, wants to feel his heart crush between his ears as this handsome stud consumes him, as he gives himself over. The taste of tequila and sativa swirl around in their mouths as the water churns around them.

"I can't stop myself," the hunk says. "I'm sorry, but you're just too much to resist."

Finally, Dylan pulls himself away, his breath coming in gulps and gasps, chest heaving as if he's run a marathon. He skims over to the other side of the tub, trying to contain himself, contain the world, unable to prevent the smile twisting the corners of his mouth. Again, his eyes meet the hunk's, water like raindrops and tears drip from their lashes, wisps of steam like ghosts coil around their faces.

They launch, the two of them, as if someone waved a checkered flag, water rushing toward and away and around as they slam chests together in the center of the tub, now grabbing and gripping every part, hands on nipples, balls, cocks like swords battering away. Legs wrapping and unwrapping as they float on each other, mouths and faces pressed together, tasting, licking, exploring, lips scruffing against beard and cheek.

Hands knead mounds of cheeks, fingers explore cracks, poking and probing, delicate then rough, an eddy of legs and arms and bodies entwining and unraveling over and again in braids and knots. Now together lifting out of the water, water spilling over, bodies pouring onto the smooth wooden deck, fish flopping on a peer, soft flesh, hard wood (of all kinds) pushing and prodding. What is up or down and who is doing what?

Dylan feels himself grow dizzy, the heat, the wrestling, the margaritas all spiraling through his brain. *Maybe we should stop* he thinks as he pulls the furry wet man toward him, biting through beard to chin, teeth accidentally clicking, electric jolts searing through every inch of his skull, down to his toes.

Now he's pinned down, the other man, much shorter, but strong, so strong, his knees happily rolling across biceps, the round cheeks working their way down, as if they could grab his stomach, hold it in place. He closes his eyes, allows himself to breathe it all in, to let loose and relish the feel of it, the momentousness of it, the fantasy of a life he never thought he'd live, not before when sweating it out in a desert, or behind those pale antiseptic drapes, or home, a boy on a falling-down porch, watching kids on broken scooters. Was this really happening?

A familiar snap brings him to, his eyes open, he feels something caress his penis, a hand massaging soft silk over his erection, and he looks up into the face, the slightly gray chin, a funny smile, a boy's grin on a Hollywood star's face – slightly gap-toothed, but pure, eyes twinkling.

"Manliness is not all swagger and mountain climbing. It's also tenderness." The hunk eases himself slowly onto Dylan's now-sheathed cock, just the tip.

Finally, as if emerging from a dream, Dylan feels his senses return, his reason. He smiles. "Do you always say such weird stuff?"

The hunk (Seth, he's sure that's what he said) closes his eyes, lifts his chin toward the darkening sky. Dylan allows his hands to trace their way up, up from the groin, caressing muscles wrapped in furry flesh, up toward pecs like armor, nipples like proud soldiers.

Now their eyes meet again, that boy's smile. "I'm sorry, can't help but quote movies. One of my little tics. " And eyes close again, waiting for a signal from a god or spirit of the woods.

Dylan feels himself absorbed into the hot, tight darkness of this man, this gorgeous specimen of maturity.

Finally a sigh, and the hunk opens his eyes, grins like he's won a prize. "There you are!"

They freeze like that for a moment, a man mounted on his horse.

The hunk reaches forward, rubs the soft monkey-brush of Dylan's hair, fingers tracing their way down his cheeks. Dylan bites the finger and arches his back up off the deck, pushing himself in a bit more.

The hunk gasps, releases himself gently…easy…easy.

"Magic," the hunk says, hand tracing its way down Dylan's neck, across his shoulders down his arm, stopping and swirling over his tattoo, over the Marine insignia's eagle wings, around the globe, then resting below, on the newly branded flesh.

"Blake," he says. Just that. "Blake."

The word hangs, suspended over the mist from the tub, tipping and twirling. Goosebumps again. But no follow up question, no prying, no demand for an explanation. No "who" or "what" or "why?"

Just the word Blake, dispersing into the air. A whisper. A promise.

Blake.

The hunk leans back, pulling Dylan up with him, his hands now moving from hip to thigh to calf.

"Don't." Dylan says. "Please. It's awful."

Hands find the scarred flesh, the remnants of stitches and shrapnel and diesel burns. The fingers move delicately, reading the fleshy Braille of a story Dylan never dares tell, can't force himself to repeat.

Now the hunk takes his face in his hands, tender, understanding hands that cup his cheeks, fingers that probe the drops from his eyes. Not drips from the tub this time, not from the water. Delicate kisses on the mouth, on the eyelids, on the forehead.

Dylan feels bombs detonate, he can take it no more. With every ounce of strength he lifts them both up, rescuing them both from unseen fires and flames and explosions. The smaller man succumbs, allows himself to be handled, impaled like this on the bigger, stronger Marine. And down they go, together, he will protect them both, he will free them.

On the chaise lounge now, on top, welcoming the soft terry cloth cushions as he thrusts himself hopelessly into the hunk, each plunge eliciting another gasp. He is saving them, saving them both, liberating every ounce of his man, his buddy, getting it right this time, making it okay as he pushes, hoisting himself onto his knees, strong calves wrapping around his waist, as he saves his world.

The world spins around him, the trees rattling and undulating in the evening breeze, soft lights blinking on throughout the house, as if some fairy touched them with a wand. The blue night is a dream, the moment perfect, lust turns into a mirage of flesh.

Together they're tumbling into each other, pounding and plunging and he can feel the rumbling of that whirlpool again, of waves from the hot tub, from the distant ocean, from somewhere else, he is here and there, past and present, and he can't stop it. Their moans and gasps now twine and twist into the treetops, they are both ready to release, prepared to finish this on-going symphony.

Click.

Just a small sound, a snap. Metallic. The roiling waters of the hot tub grow silent. The cicadas and crickets calm…awaiting the next moment.

His eyes shoot open, and there, by the door, above the tub, a silver ghost, arms crossed, eyes piercing.

"Christ, Dylan, I'm cumming!" the hunk shouts to a flutter of crows.

Dylan is too, clenching eyes, trying not to see that statue in the dusk standing, judging, watching. Together they wrench with each gasp and chasm of the orgasm, plowing and heaving and jerking, again and again. Dylan hears bombs, the roar of motor, again and again, grimacing, grinning, horrified and engulfed.

Total exhaustion, swift, final, collapsing, power depleted. Down into the soft furry flesh, into a state of overwhelmed joy and grief.

He opens his eyes, now that gray ghost closer. It stands still, silent, a chiseled sculpture.

"Well," the statue says, voice warm, simple. "This is what you get up to when I'm away."

He uncrosses his arms.

The hunk's head reels, off the chaise, and a laugh, louder than their orgasmic exaltation, echoes through the hills.

Dylan rolls off the man, tries to take cover behind the arches of the pergola, hiding from a certain enemy.

"Oh, it's not you I'm mad at," the gray ghost says. He lifts his chin, indicating the splayed hunk on the chaise. "Seth you naughty boy."

Again, Dylan feels as if he's found himself on the battlefield, ambushed, another casualty.

CHAPTER THREE: RICHARD AND THE FOUR BEARS

"You should have seen it," said Seth, happy to be regaling his audience. "He silently picked up his clothes, keeping low to the ground as if dodging incoming artillery fire—"

"Not a word, as if he'd been court marshaled," Richard jumped in, as if they'd told it hundreds of times (and they had). "You could just hear the rat-a-tat-tat of the snare drum as he marched off the deck, into the woods, toward his car."

Their audience laughed appreciatively, marveling at the daring sexual exploits laid out for all to taste and enjoy. Richard stood, the lone hairless humanoid amidst a brooding pack of bears, his hairy husband and a trio of old friends, themselves part of an unconventional living arrangement. Even Seth seemed to grow in stature, his physique shape-shifting to mirror the hirsute trio draped around their back deck, all relishing the last dregs of summer (and cocktails). Three luscious bears: Mama, soft and primped, Papa, solid and sturdy, and Baby...just right. They fit so perfectly together that their mailbox even boasted a silhouette of three happy galumphing bears.

"I kind of feel sorry for the guy," Baby Bear, or Joey, said, watching the faces of the others. He stood up, his compact, sturdy body gym-toned and tanned. The others laughed even more at this. He put his glass on the wrought iron table struck a pose, hands on hips, objecting to the hilarity. "I mean, he's a Marine! Obviously battle scarred, and scaring the shit out of him hardly seems fair!"

The laugher died down, chastened and embarrassed. Mama Bear, or Chaz, pulled the furry fireplug of a man onto his lap. "There, there, so sensitive." Although Mama Bear bore a striking resemblance to Grizzly Adams, a fabled mountain man —all denim and tattered animal hides — his voice dripped like a strand of pink pearls at Christmas. His coos and cuddles, suggesting teacups and honey wafers, were at once condescending, and comforting. Baby Bear nestled himself onto Mama's lap, rested his head on his soft shoulder. Soon enough he was content, absently fiddling with Mama's waxed handlebar mustache.

"I know, I know. Don't think we didn't have pangs. He was such a lost, lovely, damaged soul." Sobered, Richard refilled glasses, allowing the echoes of their cruel joke to fade into the night. The chorus of crickets, now without their lead vocalists, consumed the silence.

"We let him in on our little ruse, explained how it all worked." Seth jumped in. "Eventually, he understood. I mean, who wouldn't need a little drama to spice up a 20-year marriage?"

Richard whipped his head around and glared.

"You're lucky he didn't kill you, tear you apart with his strong Marine arms!" This, said by Papa Bear, or Phil, as he adjusted the crotch of his shorts and patted his proud belly. The largest of the three bears, Papa was also the gentlest, at once imposing, lumbering, and gentle as a panda.

"How do you know he didn't have PTSD?" Baby Bear, still ruminating, soft, quiet. Tears rimmed his eyes, and he did indeed look a bit like a child – all 30 years of him. "This guy fought for our country."

Mama Bear patted his red head and clucked.

Richard again felt that twinge of guilt, a feeling he would never become inured to, not for this, or any number of his transgressions, real or imagined. He hung his head and wedged himself onto the lounge chair between Seth's legs.

"How do you keep your life from sounding like a party trick?" Richard asked, not really a question to the group, but perhaps a topic for an article. "I think that the older I get, the more I can feel someone's pain while simultaneously exploiting it."

Seth reached over and rubbed his head. "It's okay." Seth watched Richard carefully, waiting to react.

"No, it's not." Richard felt himself sink a little further. He often felt darkness tugging at him, relied on Seth's cheerful nature to help lift him away from its gravity. Just as often as not, Richard found himself stubbornly holding on to dismay.

"Well, I can tell you, if I ever get fucked by a studly Marine, I want to have it filmed!" Mama bear announced, breaking the momentary doldrums. He leaned in, stroking a thick, hairy thigh. "He *was* hung, wasn't he?"

"Like an anaconda!" Seth admitted. "Like a python in heat."

"Do pythons go into heat?" Papa Bear asked of no one.

For a moment, everyone pondered that one. Probably not about the python, but what the Marine was packing (truth be told).

"Who wants a steam?" Seth gently prodded Richard off the lounge, a silent command to change this dreary mood.

"I'm ready for the whole spa treatment!" Mama Bear shot off her chaise, dumping Baby Bear unceremoniously, a housewife rushing a Black Friday sale.

"Only if I can avail myself of your outdoor shower!" Papa Bear whisked off his tank top and jiggled his round, furry belly.

Seth led the two older men into the house as Richard picked up the cocktail tray and empty glasses. Baby Bear paused at the door, his baleful eyes triggering something in Richard.

"Do you think he was okay?" Baby Bear asked. "I mean, that Marine, did he forgive you? That was pretty shitty."

"Dylan. His name was Dylan." Richard put the tray down and straightened up. "It took a bit of clearing up. But we made sure he knew we were just teasing each other. By night's end, we were all snuggling in our California King."

"And what about the Donut boy?"

"Kyle," Richard wanted to address them by their names, hoping that removing the grossly unfair titles, 'The Marine,' 'The Donut Boy," he might restore some of their dignity. "I never caught up with him again. I tried, going to the takeout window a few times, but he hid in the back." He hung his head low. "I felt like a creep, like a pederast hanging around a playground."

"I worry about collateral damage." Baby Bear also hung his head in unity, something that Richard found adorable.

"I know. I want to make good." He put his arm around Baby Bear, feeling the strong shoulders beneath an enticing inch of baby fat. "You're very sweet."

Baby Bear looked up, revealing smoldering green eyes beneath red lashes. Richard, almost a head taller than the young chunk-a-dunk, pulled him in for a hug, nestling his nose into Baby Bear's bristly hair, inhaling his shampoo and gel, just that whiff of *eau'de bear.* And he couldn't help himself. Soon he was kissing Baby Bear's lips and tongue, tasting the margaritas and traces of sativa they'd been vaping. Baby Bear succumbed, allowed himself to be groped and gripped and pulled, and soon enough he too was devouring not just the mouth, but nipping at Richard's neck and ears.

They could have gone further, right then and there, as their hands, as if on cue, reached into each other's shirts to caress bellies and tweak nipples. But hearing the grumble of bears below, Richard thought better of it. Reluctantly, he pulled his lips away, leaned his forehead against Baby Bear's.

"I don't know what's fair game here."

Baby Bear's face lifted, a smile forming on his glistening lips. "We only play together, actually."

"And this constitutes…?"

"Preamble." Baby Bear pulled his striped t-shirt off over his head, walked toward the house. He opened the slider, and pulled down the back of his shorts, just enough so Richard could see the enticing red fur disappearing into the crevices of those sturdy round cheeks.

Richard looked at the tray of drinks, noted a bee buzzing around the dregs of the pitcher. "I can get this stuff later."

He followed Baby Bear into the house.

Richard took a moment after disrobing to collect extra towels and guest robes, draping them along a series of hooks on the bathroom wall. Once again, he was thrilled that they'd installed the steam shower, which had really been a lark. Who knew they'd be using it in such new and creative ways?

Seth had based the entire design on the schvitz baths of his youth in Flatbush. He had amused Richard with intriguing stories of tiled walls, flimsy white towels, and the dangling balls of Jewish men of all ages, gathering for this ancient ritual.

(They both speculated on what other activities these rituals *really* entailed.)

Richard peered into the glass door, condensation obliterating anything that moved beyond. He could hear voices, laughs, and giggles, muffled reverberations beyond the thick double-paned glass. He looked down at his skimpy underwear, the strained pouch already giving way to his mounting excitement, and peeled them off. He adjusted the dimmer for the light inside the steamroom, only slightly, revealing rolling mounds of pink, rosy flesh, refracted in the rivulets of water running down the glass.

He jumped when a wet palm slammed against the door, then another, as grunts and groans followed. Things, and bears, were heating up.

"Back up, I'm coming in boys," he announced as he turned the handle and slipped in, retaining as much of the thick steam as possible.

Inside, he could make out unfocused shapes writhing and undulating. The slurps and moans amidst the steady whoosh of the steam conjured all sorts of images, painting on the blank canvas of fog. The room smelled of eucalyptus and sweat, reminding him of his own encounters in the steam room of the NY Sports Club – an instant boner maker.

His depth perception was shot, as he blindly felt his way through the white clouds, groping toward the sounds, imagining a tangle of bodies twisting and rolling along the tiled seating tiers only a foot or so away. A step closer, and the moans echoed, became visible as phantoms in the churning fog.

Hands, fingers long and meaty, grabbed him by the butt, yanked him into the heaving mountain of wooly grizzlies. A mouth found its way to his inner thigh, worked its way across his loins, teasing his delicates, slithering down below and between and around. He leaned back and sighed, loud, free, joining the on-going musical refrain of ursine singing. Reaching out, he found a thick back hunched over like a buffalo at a watering hole. Like Helen Keller, his fingers traced the round, broad shoulders, across the chunky neck, discovering Mama Bear's drenched coils, over his furrowed forehead to find the nose disappearing between two muscular mounds.

He knew that shape anywhere, had learned every curve and dimple night after night for over 20 years. He helped spread open his husband's thick cheeks, allowing Mama Bear access to the treasures deep within.

Suddenly, he felt his erection being sucked into a warm, hot vortex of an eager, skilled mouth. He turned toward the pleasure, allowed himself to be consumed from below, when his own mouth and throat were surprised by the sudden arrival an impressive endowment. He inhaled deeply to discover a foreign fragrance, lavender and musk mixed with a salty taste that only made him thrust forward and back, head and hips bucking in their own private watusi. *A little choking, a few tears, not bad*, he thought.

Now several hands slipped across his smooth, hot skin as he groped and pulled at bristled hair and short, slicked curls, across and around happy stomachs and generous tits. The moaning grew thick and guttural, like hungry pigs at the trough. He'd heard men utter these sounds once before, when he had found himself, inadvertently (don't ask) under the "dick dock" in Provincetown during Bear Week, where men performed ancient sacraments in the dark, in the sand.

The air grew too heavy, the tangle of arms and limbs and mouths dizzying. He groped his way across the wall, found a switch and pressed, happy to hear the steam jets halt, only the grunting and snorting echoing throughout this tiled grotto. He thought of himself as the foundling child, raised by a pack of wild animals, steeped in their language and actions, but always a foreigner, an outsider.

He heard a familiar click and a crank from the other side as Seth opened the window in the back of the room. Richard stepped back, reached behind and opened the opposing window. The steam retreated, rushing out into the night, revealing a heap of beefy men, blinking and confused in the clear, cool air.

"Water!" Seth called out, winking at Richard.

Richard would have blushed, the way he did every time his adorable husband smiled at him that way, but he was already flushed red from head to toe.

* * *

The mats Seth had recently procured proved to be a good investment, as the bears played leap frog over and around and through in their workout room. Richard tried to keep up with condoms and lube and towels, referee to a rowdy wrestling match.

Mama Bear was the first to refuse the wrapper, then Papa, followed by Baby.

"We're all tested and Tru!" Papa announced, referring to the daily dosage of Truvada, the (dangerously misinterpreted) miracle drug that finally permitted gay men to let their guard down, to stop worrying. After years of panic each time a condom broke, each over-eager slip-up that had sent them into anxious tailspins, a new breed of homo was emerging: stupid and randy lunatics, harking back to the care-free seventies.

"There are other things to worry about," Richard warned, accepting his role as the wet blanket. "Think of the many STIs—"

Seth pressed a finger to his lips, halting a well-prepared monologue. Sweeping Richard up into his arms, his thick erection, pressed between Richard's thighs. He grabbed Richards face in his hands, his signature gesture, stared deeply into his eyes and said, "Let's not worry. Not tonight." He covered Richard's mouth with his own, before he could protest. Together they inhaled deeply, their tongues twisting together, announcing their own truce.

Richard released his mouth, pulled back to take in Seth's eager, accepting brown eyes. As if on cue, the three bears halted their lovemaking, and gathered, on hands and knees, around the couple. Richard felt like an innocent, a child, vulnerable and nervous, his determined erection now straining so hard in excitement that he thought the head might pop off.

"Okay?" Seth asked quietly.

Richard looked up, enamored of that childlike grin, that trusting faith. He nodded shyly.

Seth kissed his forehead, turned to the bears, and smiled. Gently, he lowered Richard into their waiting arms, gleefully sacrificing his lover to an eager, hungry horde.

Richard gave in, allowed himself to be feasted upon, surrendering his senses, his worries, his stress, his inhibitions. Submitting himself to the gorgeous, untamed wildlife now gulping away, he relished every poke and prod of his flesh. He succumbed completely, was opened up, explored inside and out, yielding to fingers and mouths, prying hands, thrusting bodies.

Was this how Goldilocks felt? He didn't know. But better or worse, this felt *juuust riiight.*

* * *

Richard and his sated bears sprawled around the living room; Papa Bear, head in Mama's lap, Baby Bear nestling alongside Richard on the deep leather sofa. Seth busied himself with refreshments, a smorgasbord of nibbles materializing on the Eames coffee table before them. Plush white robes teased at the tantalizing bits of flesh and fur, as each happy camper hummed and sighed with satisfaction.

Seth, swirling brandy in a snifter, alighted on his swan chair and stretched out. "I'd say that's another night for the books. Thanks for sharing, boys!"

Richard mindlessly brushed Baby Bear's hair back and forth, twirling his fingers around his apricot-shaped ears, across his thick bearded jaw. "Usually bears only play with other bears."

Baby Bear reached up, gently stroking Richard's cheek and looking into his eyes. "You've got so much more to offer than meat and fur!"

"I say you're more than equipped to trap your share of bears!" Papa Bear laughed and squeezed Mama's stomach.

"How do you do it?" Seth asked, watching strands of amber brandy climb down the snifter. "How do you keep all of it fair and equal? The three of you act together, moving through life as a team."

"We communicate, darling," Mama said, scooting Papa off his lap. "We hash it all out. It's not that hard."

"Don't you get jealous?"

The happy bears exchanged glances and laughed.

"That's half the fun of it!" Papa Bear grabbed Mama and smashed his face against his, and the two continued to lick and rub beards back and forth.

Richard peered over at Seth, who couldn't meet his eye. This time he did blush.

"You're so cute!" Baby Bear reached up and pulled Richard toward him.

Richard couldn't help but smile. "Well, you are the perfect throuple, I will say that."

"You make it look easy." Seth raised his snifter and toasted his guests.

"Well, what ever happened to your little twink?" Mama asked. "What was his name?"

"Twink won't cut it," Richard said, suddenly defensive for the ex-lover. "We ain't Daddies; he ain't no twink."

Baby Bear sat up, almost reprimanding Mama like a true adolescent. "Daniel! His name is Daniel."

"Daniel," the others repeated, as Richard and Seth exchanged freighted looks.

"You were together since before these two found me," Baby said. "In fact, I think you were their role models."

The others nodded and grunted in agreement.

Seth ran his finger along the rim of his glass. "We didn't know you knew."

This proved to be the laugh line of the night, with the three bears guffawing in unison.

"The whole WORLD knew!" Mama said, nodding his head vigorously.

"Don't tell me it was a secret!" Papa Bear sounded incredulous. "I mean, you guys were like the gay Marx Brothers, with your own little language and routines. Who could miss it?"

Richard stood up, ready for this night to end. "Let's just say there were complications. Who wants something else? I'm bushed."

"Hey, you don't get to change the subject like that, spill." Papa grunted.

"Yeah, spill."

"Spill."

Richard disappeared behind the bar, clinking glasses, looking for another snifter, one big enough to either hide behind or drown in.

Wrapping his robe around his outstretched legs, Seth explained, as much as he could, about the downfall of their own little throuple. How they were all doing just fine, until they discovered that not only had Daniel been videotaping them, but posting them on the web. He omitted salient details that many of the videos were consensual, focusing instead on the betrayal. He painted Richard and himself as innocent victims caught up in a nefarious plot.

When all was laid out before them, the bears could only shake their heads.

"We had no idea."

"That's terrible."

"You got copies of the videos?" Papa Bear asked with a winking leer.

Richard polished off the last of his brandy. "Well, it's all Britta under the bridge. He's gone. The website is down, the videos destroyed…"

"Or so we've been told."

"And the little shit is history." He stood and reached out so Seth could take his hand. After helping him up, he pulled his husband in close. "Sometimes you get lucky…"

"And sometimes that luck runs out." Seth yawned dramatically. "And with that, this little bear is bushed."

The bears murmured their sad regrets, gathered their clothes, and with a minimum of discussion, made their way upstairs. Richard led them out, standing on the front deck to see them off to their car. He lingered, thinking of Daniel, of the guest room, of the secrets and lies, about all of it. He heard footsteps approach and looked up to see Baby Bear.

"I couldn't leave without another kiss," Baby Bear said, pulling him down, pushing his tongue into Richard's welcoming mouth. Although Richard was ready to stop, Baby held him tighter, squeezing him. Richard wanted to cry, wanted to apologize to the world for everything he'd done wrong. As if sensing all of this, Baby Bear squeezed harder.

At last Richard pulled away. Baby Bear held his face close and whispered. "Maybe over isn't really over?" He brushed Richard's face with the back of his hand. "Maybe you all have room for forgiveness."

Richard saw trusting hope in that sweet face. Before he could respond, Baby Bear skidaddled to the awaiting car, and they drove off. He watched as the car turned around, the red taillights disappearing down the hill, two devil eyes swallowed by the woods.

The looming creatures of the night, the metallic chirp of the crickets, the rattle of the cicadas, the owls and toads and nighthawks, all screeched and shrieked in an enormous crescendo. Richard fell to his knees as tears splashed onto the wooden deck. He rode the tidal crash of sadness, self-pity, anger, sobbing until he was spent, crumpled, alone, and desolate in the furious cacophony of the night.

What had he done? What had he lost?

Book Two:
The Spare Dick

Voicemail

Richard
Mobile

Transcription Beta (low confidence)

"Hey hum it's me I won't get out of the city pill late probably eat something on the train you know a slice of pizza or whatever god the city is awful tonight okay anyway I'll see you when I see you…"

Was this transcription useful or not useful

Daniel
Mobile

Transcription Beta (low confidence)

"I know you still hate me but I really need help desperately a sap if you could call please okay hope you get this…"

Was this transcription useful or not useful

CHAPTER FOUR: THE DANIEL SADS

"Fuck-piss-goddamn-mother-cocksucker-twat-lick-shit-ass-fuck!" Seth tossed the crowbar and lug wrench, clinking and clanking, onto the driveway. "Fuck fuck fuck fuck."

Daniel, inured to Seth's rare, but explosive fits of rage, sighed, walked over and picked up the tools.

"When was the last time you changed this fucking piece of shit tire? I swear the lug nuts are welded to the wheel."

Daniel crouched down next to him and put his hand on his sweat-drenched shoulders. "It's been a while." He put the tools gently on the asphalt next to Seth, inhaling deeply, perhaps just to calm down. "It's not like I get a flat every other day. Maybe I should practice more often."

Seth laughed at that, finally releasing his anger and frustration. "Tell you what, let me call Triple A, and we'll have it done the right way." He looked up into Daniel's blue eyes and felt an old, familiar flutter.

"It's not your car," Daniel said. "Will they fix it?"

"I dunno." He pulled out his phone. "They will when I add you to the family plan."

* * *

Seth stepped into Daniel's apartment, happy for the air conditioning, as loud and rickety as it was. He watched Daniel glide ahead, as if he were walking on water. God, how he'd missed watching that ass, how he'd missed...*forget it. Just forget it.*

"I only have Costco tequila mix, if that's okay," he called out from the kitchenette. "I'd offer you water but my pipes are rusty. Don't want you to catch tetanus."

Seth looked around the apartment, once again shocked by how small it was, how confining. The entire thing would fit in their living room. In New York they would have called it an "L-shaped" studio. In Connecticut it was a crack-house efficiency. Everywhere he looked dirty clothes were flung and draped, as if a hamper exploded. The bed, really just a mattress on the floor, was covered by a dingy, thread-worn sheet. His computer sat on a crate by the bed, an industrial-sized pump bottle of lube nearby. All around lay discarded beer cans, empty Cuervo bottles, the occasional can of black beans with a bent spoon or fork sticking out. He couldn't help feel disgusted, but not just at the condition of the apartment. He was responsible for Daniel's sad state of affairs; he and Richard had made sure that Daniel was busted to nothing. In addition to taking away his job, they made sure he was bankrupted by legal bills that would haunt him the rest of his life. At the time of the lawsuits, they felt vindicated. Daniel had betrayed them, publicly and viciously.

But now, looking at the desolation of Daniel's life, he couldn't help but feel guilty.

"Sorry it's warm, I don't want to make ice out of tetanus water either," Daniel handed Seth a ball jar with piss-colored liquid.

"Yeah, tetanus gives you lockjaw." Seth inspected the suspicious, oddly viscous contents in the jar.

"Lockjaw would be career suicide!" Daniel's laugh sounded awkward and forced.

Seth pressed the jar to his lips, but dared only a sip.

"Anyway, thanks for coming over. I couldn't find anyone else to help, and I knew you'd be nearby."

They stood in the middle of the apartment, awkwardly appraising each other, like two strangers in an elevator.

"Well...thanks. For the help. And the Triple A membership."

"Yeah, well, I couldn't..." his voice trailed off as he again looked at the squalid conditions in which Daniel was living. "You can't go around without any road service. Not with your old clunker."

"Yeah, well, the bookstore doesn't quite pay enough for that new Beemer I've been looking at." Again, the laugh sounded forced.

Seth snorted appreciatively, but it wasn't a laugh. Just punctuation.

"Anyway, thanks again. I guess I'll...well you know. Whatever." He turned away from Seth and paused for a moment. Not looking back, he said "I gotta hit the shower. Get ready for work. You can let yourself out, right?"

Seth watched Daniel stride toward the bathroom. "Yeah, well...take care of yourself."

He walked the few steps to the door, ready to turn the knob and leave, but thought he should say something else. When he turned back, he was startled to see Daniel shirtless and stepping out of his cargo shorts. He dropped his head in shame and left.

Standing in the hallway of the apartment building, its walls cracked, floors caked with ancient dust and grime, the air redolent of cat piss and vomit, he felt small and ugly. This wouldn't do. This was not who he was. Not who they were. He shook his head, turned around, swung the door open and marched back in, through the laundry-strewn room and into the bathroom.

"This isn't right. I'm sorry." He yanked the dingy shower curtain open, revealing Daniel's compact, sinewy body, his charming farmer's tan and enticingly soaped crotch.

"Well hello d'ere!" Daniel said in that silly voice he adopted in situations like this, a voice Seth had missed for almost a year now.

For once in a blue moon (whenever that might be), Seth was speechless. Looking at his ex-lover, his slippery smooth skin, slicked back hair, and protruding protrusion, he forgot what he was going to say.

For his part, Daniel just stood there, wiped the soap out of his eyes, and waited.

"Fuck it." Seth kicked off his sandals, stepped out of his shorts, tore off his shirt, and stepped into the shower. He grabbed Daniel by the face, held it tight, fell into those cerulean eyes, and began to cry. He wanted to kiss him, wanted to taste his sweet breath, feel his plump lips.

Instead he burst out crying.

"Hey, it's okay," Daniel said, reaching around Seth's waist and pulling him close, pressing Seth's head to his shoulder. "It's okay."

"I'm sorry. I'm sorry. I'm so sorry." He gasped back tears, but the water streaming into his face made him choke. The hacking convulsed, ugly heaving bawling bowed him, spittle running down his chin, spiraling down the drain with water and soap. Daniel rubbed his back, kneeled next to him, and borrowed a move from Seth's book. He grabbed him by the jaw with both hands and smiled gently, gazing into his face.

"It's okay, hon." He pressed his lips against Seth's, just a touch. "I was a real asshat. It's me who should be begging your forgiveness. When all the shit went down, I just got so fucking obstinate."

Seth, his breath returning, nodded his head. He couldn't tell if he was still crying, or the shower was just streaming from his eyes. He blinked back the water, staring at that familiar face that had cut a hole into his world, carved out a piece of his heart, and fought back another wave of sobs.

Daniel smoothed the hair on Seth's forehead and pulled him closer, his soap-slicked hands gliding up and down his bristly back.

As if they hadn't skipped a day, a minute, a beat, their mouths found each other, their hands groped, massaged, and slid around in a choreography embedded in every cell of their bodies. The tight confines of the fiberglass tub gave them little room to move, knees and shins compressed, skin grinding into bone, but they didn't care. Hands explored skin and muscles, buttocks and thighs, backs, searching their way through memories and fantasies long since veiled by anger and sadness.

Daniel groped behind Seth, in search of something on the edge of the tub. Losing his balance, he fell forward, and the two tumbled onto Seth's back with a hollow thud.

"I'm sorry – ouch! Did that hurt?"

Seth didn't answer, just pulled the smaller man on top of himself as if the running warm water would help him draw this missing piece of his soul back into his flesh.

Daniel retrieved a bottle of lotion and squirted it recklessly across their chests and stomachs, grinding it into Seth's swirls of fur, using Seth as his own full-body loofah.

Seth arched his back as Daniel's slippery hands wandered their way to his groin, guiding his own hands to the soft but strong mounds of Daniel's cheeks. He spread them open and allowed his fingers to tickle the soft hairs, occasionally finding that extra something, sending an electric jolt through his long-lost lover, a zap that radiated through both of them, as if he'd grabbed a live power line.

Daniel tried to lower himself onto Seth, his hands slipping and sliding, ready to take aim, but then finding it elusive, slipping away.

Again and again, their bodies ground against each other, almost there, then having it all slip away. Tantalizing and desperately frustrating.

"Stop, stop," Seth called out. "Turn off the water. Just…" He gently pushed Daniel off and slid up the back of the tub.

Daniel reached back and shut off the shower. "I'm sorry."

"No, please. No sorry. I just can't." He tried to get up, but the lotion had made the entire tub like a luge course and they were taking a treacherous turn.

Without a word, Daniel grabbed a couple of towels, tossed one onto Seth's chest, and wrapped the other around himself.

Fuck, Seth thought. *Just fuck.* He hadn't planned on this, hadn't even expected it. Daniel's call had caught him off guard in more ways than one. He watched Daniel's strong legs step over the side of the tub, a long-forgotten lump in his throat revealing itself. It had never gone away.

He looked up at the outstretched hand, almost wilted when he felt the coarse worker's skin, the sturdy grip. He looked up into Daniel's eyes peering out from that lovely face, soft, trusting. Standing proved to be a challenge, the tub itself coated with a slick of body lotion.

"Easy does it," Daniel said as he hiked a shoulder under Seth's arm. Together they limped out of the tub.

At last sure of his footing, Seth pulled the towel across his back and stepped out of the claustrophobic bathroom. He couldn't bring himself to face Daniel. "It's not that I don't want to. Not that

I haven't daydreamed about it for almost a full year. I really just can't. Not today." Now thoughts of Richard clouded his head, eliciting a stabbing, shameful sense of betrayal.

"I understand." Daniel followed Seth out of the room. They grew silent as they toweled themselves off.

Seth turned back to look at Daniel, who had pulled into the corner of the room. Again, that satiny smooth back, those compact muscles, sculpted shoulders. "Let me help you." He toweled the water off Daniel's back, the way he'd done so many times before. In better times. In better homes.

He felt something roaring from deep in the pit of his stomach, a momentous growl that he'd suppressed, that he'd almost forgotten he owned. It was like a concerto he'd long since forgotten had erupted from an orchestra he'd thought lost. Each muscle in his body flexed, stood at attention, and he felt himself growing another foot. He grabbed Daniel by the shoulders, spun him around, grabbed him by the face, and kissed him deeply.

After what felt like a blessed eternity, he reared back, looked into the surprisingly bashful eyes, and laughed. "The truth is, I just don't have the right equipment with me. You know…" He felt himself blush.

Daniel smiled.

Ever since his surgery, Seth had relied on injections to give himself full erections. He no longer kept an emergency supply in his glove compartment. What would be the point?

"It's okay."

Seth straightened his shoulder and felt himself beaming, a smile that he'd thought had been lost forever. "Oh, I know it's okay. It's more than okay."

He swung Daniel around, with welcome ferocity. Together they toppled over onto the mattress.

"There's more than one way to skin a cat!" Seth straddled his former lover's strong torso, reached behind, grabbed Daniel in a way he'd longed for, and in one sweeping moment, brought himself down, his insides bursting in paroxysms of pain and joy, an ecstasy that ignited every nerve in his body. He felt the wonders of Daniel as he rode the thunderous bliss.

"I may have been a bad Boy Scout," he gasped. "But I'm always prepared in my own way."

He rode Seth's bucking hips like a broncobuster. He was Wyatt Earp, a Remington sculpture, Deborah Winger in Urban Fucking Cowboy!

* * *

Seth leaned on one arm, tracing the silky hairs that sprouted around Daniel's button-like nipples. Golden sunlight, peeping through tattered and bent mini-blinds, raked across their bare torsos. The steady rush of late afternoon traffic, the croaks of passing semi-trucks, the wheeze of air brakes drowned out their contented sighs. By now they communicated far beyond words as they drank each other in.

Daniel reached up and brushed Seth's beard, his finger finding a buried dimple. "Remember that hike we used to take up Cockaponset Park? The one with the clearing and hidden deer canopy?"

Seth smiled, his eyes glancing to the left as he recalled several happy sojourns. "How can I forget?"

"I went there the other day, on a whim."

"I haven't been since…" He cocked his head. "Since you."

"It wasn't the same."

"No hot young stud to keep you company?"

"Hardly."

Seth flopped onto his back, and they lay quietly, shoulder to shoulder, the heat from their exertions stinging like sunburn as they touched.

"I actually snapped my carrot in the bushes, but I couldn't cum."

Seth surprised himself with the intensity of his laughter. For some reason it seemed ridiculously appropriate, sad, and wonderful. "Snapped your carrot. So vivid! We'll have to fix that," he said, fresh tears of joy on his cheeks. "Won't we?"

"Hmmm." Daniel sighed, long and loud, before nuzzling his nose into Seth's armpit. In moments they both drifted into heavenly sleep.

In his dream he heard himself say: *Don't tell Richard, don't tell Richard, Don't tell Richard.*

Caller unknown
Mobile

Transcription Beta (low confidence)

"You thought you could save yourself didn't you Seth well we all see how that worked out didn't we before long _____ will know and _____ _____ by then it will be all over town your ass on the line and that's not all just wait just wait and see what's in store for you…"

Was this transcription useful or not useful

CHAPTER FIVE: JACKIE

"No, the brownie is for when you finish the article," Jackie told herself, eyeing the rich, dark treat on the edge of her desk. She could smell the chocolate, the walnuts, could just about feel the surge of dopamine as the sugar flooded her brain. For now, those reward receptors would just have to wait until she finished her article for *Psychology Today* (or as she called it, *Psychosomatic Today*, because only laymen and nutjobs looked at the rag).

Before she could even begin typing (or spewing, because she'd been writing the article in her head for a whole week), she had to get her hair out of her face. Where had she left her hair clip? As she opened and slammed all of her desk drawers in succession, her gaze continued to fall on that evil brownie.

Picking at a corner (just a crumb), she looked around the room, wondering where in hell any one of the dozens of hair clips she bought and lost must be. But the office was neat as a hairpin (ha ha). She was due for a cut and a color, and her mane of curls was blossoming in the late-summer humidity.

Just one more bit of brownie (just to warm up); she looked around her desk in dismay. At long last, her eyes fell on a stack of papers held together by a binder clip. Well, fuck, who was going to see her anyway? Yanking the clip off with one hand, she coiled her hair up into a messy knot at the top of her head and pinched the clip over it.

She grabbed the brownie and nibbled at the edge, a reward for her ingenuity.

Now the article: she sat at the desk and looked at the blank screen on her computer. Why wasn't this any easier? Maybe just another nibble of the brownie would help. *Just a little, I'm serious.*

As she stared into her computer, into her own brain, she wondered if the article made any difference. "Infidelity in the workplace" was hardly a topic that needed any more coverage. Yeah, the number one place for affairs was the workplace, and not some "me too" moment, but affairs between equals, consenting adults. Check. Holiday office parties: a hotbed of potential for inter-office affairs. Check. The article Jackie really wanted to write was: "Fidelity in the workplace: admit to your spouse you're horny and want to schtup your colleague."

The sight of the brownie beckoning her from the edge of her desk distracted. Rather than continue whittling away at it, she would just shove it in the drawer and retrieve it later. *That's it. But just one more bite.*

She opened the drawer, dropped the brownie in. Slam. *Ouch goddamn!* She shook out her banged up finger.

"Brownies in the workplace can be dangerous," she typed. "Overeating in the workplace…" she added. Despite her helpless staring, the computer offered up no ideas. A calendar alert popped up on her screen.

"Appointment: Darryl 4 p.m."

Who the hell is Darryl? And why did Pilar schedule something when she had specifically requested to keep this time open for writing? This was the problem with having an assistant, one she'd never met, working from Mexico City. She was ready to type something furious in a text, but realized that the time difference screwed them both up. Opening the bottom desk drawer (not the one with the brownie) and glancing through her files she confirmed that she had never had a client named Darryl.

Oy. She hated starting with a new client when she felt under pressure. So she'd better get herself together. She got up from her desk, did a quick forward bend, a slow rise to standing (namasté hands), and repeated, getting more into her body, more into her breath. Upon standing tall the third time, she spotted the clock and realized it was 4:05. Shit. She never kept anyone waiting.

"Darryl?" she asked as she opened the door and peered into the shared waiting room. An odd assortment of adults of all shapes and sizes looked from Jackie to each other, then back to their laps, phones, or magazines. She'd witnessed this phenomenon before: psychiatric patients scanning the room, hoping nobody they know was there, but curious to see who might be sicker.

"Darryl?" she asked again, and again the curious looked around, then back to Jackie and then finally to their laps. She was about to close the door when she felt the floors shake, as someone bounded up the stairs. A sandy haired young man, strapping in his tank top and baggy white shorts, turned the corner and took the final stairs two at a time.

"Jackie?" the young man asked, pausing to catch his breath. "Sorry I'm late."

Jackie felt the world somersault. This had to be a mistake. "Daniel?"

"I talked to Pilar, she put me down for 4."

Oh shit. Now she really would have to talk to Pilar. First of all, the name thing was inexcusable, and second, she could at least have filled a bit in on the intake questionnaire before scheduling someone that she had no intention in treating. For any reason.

"Come in," she said, holding the door open, smiling at the others in the waiting room as they shifted in their seats.

"Good to see you," Daniel offered a hand, but Jackie avoided it, busying herself with closing the door. "You look beautiful today."

"I can't treat you," she said as she closed the door. "I thought you'd know that. I can't even speak to you professionally."

"I figured."

"And what's more," she said, striding to her desk, "I can't speak to you personally either. Not after everything you did."

"I didn't know who else to call."

"How about the police?"

Daniel laughed, shook his head. "I always admired your sense of humor."

"I wasn't joking." Jackie sat down on her Aeron chair and punched some keys on her computer. There it was. Pilar *had* taken an intake form. Boyfriend problems. Anxiety. Why hadn't she seen it sooner? Was misnomer Darryl Pilar's mistake? Or had Daniel done that on purpose?

"You have every right to be mad, I understand, I do."

Jackie turned her chair to face Daniel. She took a moment to look him up and down, taking in the full, sculpted shoulders, the thick ropy biceps, the man cleavage…and of course those deadly blue eyes. No wonder her best friends had fallen for him. If he hadn't been a psychopath, she too might have been smitten. Anyone with a functioning libido would want this guy. Especially the way those Disney-prince eyes took you in, that slight smile, perfect teeth looking all wholesome and sweet.

Daniel sat on the edge of the leather chair – her chair! – clasped his hands over his knees. "Jackie, I know you're mad, and I promise you, I wouldn't dream of bothering you, but I think I'm falling apart, and I don't know where to turn." He hung his head, slouched forward. "I've just been a wreck."

Jackie looked away, unwilling to give in. Ever since the whole affair with Richard and Seth had blown up, all of the uploaded videos exposed, the lies, the cheating, the lawsuits, the late nights when she and her husband Aaron consoled their best friends, she wanted nothing to do with Daniel.

And now he was crying. Sitting in her chair, sobbing like an infant. She got up, grabbed the box of tissues and thrust it at him.

"Thank you."

"You're in my chair."

"Oh, so sorry." He jumped out of the seat, looking around.

"Go ahead, sit on the couch."

"Should I lie down?"

"I'm not Freud."

Daniel perched on the edge of the sofa. "Thank you for seeing me."

"But I'm *not* seeing you, and really, I have nothing to say to you. Nothing you'd want to hear."

"I heard it all," he said, collapsing into the couch, another torrent of tears and snot. "Most of it I told myself."

"Well, that's your first step anyway." She sat on her leather chair, once again facing a crying person in crisis. How many of those sat on that couch? How many times had she listened to stories told through tears? How often did she have to fight off her own emotions, sorrow, sadness, and disgust? How hard did she have to dig for her nascent senses of empathy and compassion? And, once again, this blue-eyed devil was drawing out her maternal side. He didn't look like a criminal at all (how many of them did?), but a sad, broken boy.

When Daniel blew his nose, it sounded like a French horn. Jackie sat quietly while his sobs subsided. When finally he looked up at her, she just raised her eyebrows, allowing the silence to speak.

Daniel smiled slightly, his cheeks wet. "Ever since…well, ever since it's all gone down, I haven't been doing too well."

"Would you like me to refer you to someone?" She grabbed her iPhone and scrolled through her contact list.

"No – no. I actually came here as a friend."

"We aren't friends."

"But we were," he said, tilting his head like a cocker spaniel. "We had been."

"I went along with it, for Richard and Seth's sake. They saw something in you…" She held up her hand. "I'm not going to get drawn into this. I have work to do, and you've already upset my day."

Daniel looked out the window, gazing at the trees and old Victorian houses across the street. "I was thinking of those times at your home. In your hot tub, the three of us bouncing around naked with you and Aaron, drunk on mescal and pot, and it was one of my favorite memories."

"Dr. David James has an office down the street. I can give you a referral."

"I wasn't raised with money," Daniel said, looking at his palms. "My Dad left when I was ten. My mother drank. My older sister practically raised me—"

"Connie England is downstairs, she's got a great reputation with sociopaths, psychotic narcissists…"

"And I had to scrape my way through the world. It wasn't easy."

"…the criminally insane…"

"Fuck, Jackie, I need you to tell Richard that I'm sorry. I know what I did was stupid. I know it was insensitive and unforgivable, but I can't live with myself."

Jackie closed her eyes and leaned on her elbow. She felt the beginning of a headache.

"I'll pay you for the hour. I don't care. I just need you to tell me how I can fix this. You're Richard's best friend, he trusts you."

She looked back at Daniel, who had now slid down on the couch, his legs stretched in front of him. Unfortunately, that also opened up the leg of his shorts, and she could see – honest to fucking God – the tip of his penis.

"Look, I can't help you with Richard. I can't listen to your problems. I can't even be in the same room with you."

Daniel shifted again in the couch. Why the hell wasn't he wearing underwear?

"There's a liars anonymous support group online. Several of them. Why don't you start there? Steps 8, 9, and 10 might prove to be beneficial."

"Okay, okay," he crossed his ankles, and now it looked like his whole penis was going to flop out. And there was a lot to flop out; it didn't take a dip in the hot tub to know that. "Would Aaron talk to me? Guy to guy?"

"I can't speak for my husband." Jackie looked at his crotch as if mesmerized. That was his major asset, that and those bedeviling eyes. She struggled to lift her gaze to meet his, but that proved even more dangerous. Something about those deep blue orbs sucked anyone in, like a vortex. Obviously she saw what Richard and Seth had seen in him, who wouldn't?

Daniel heaved himself out of the low-slung couch, shoved his hands in his pockets.

God, you could feast on that for days, Jackie thought, then shook the notion away.

"How much do I owe you?" He pulled out his wallet and thumbed through an assortment of small bills.

"Nothing. Just go." She stood and walked to the door, turned back, only to see him adjust his crotch.

"You'll tell Richard I stopped by?"

"No. Yes. Probably."

Daniel smiled at that. It was a well-known fact that she and Richard told each other everything. *Everything*.

He walked to the doorway, turned, and leaned on it, casual, nonchalant. "So maybe I'll call Aaron?"

"Do what you'd like."

"Okay," he nodded his head, now all hang dog. "Thank you for being so decent with me."

"Fuck that."

"And…" he pointed to her hair. "Nice clip. Very becoming."

She reached up, felt the binder clip, and shoved him with the door. "I was working in here!" She yelled out suddenly. A half-dozen oddballs turned and looked at her. Daniel smiled and waved. She watched his butt as he walked away, two perfect melons twisting in a bag.

Fuck.

Where was that brownie?

Roger
Mobile

Transcription Beta (low confidence)

"Daniel this is Roger um Rodrigo from the _____ its been a month I know but please call me its important I know you have the number please call ASAP seriously this is really ducked up and I need to talk to you have been sick or anything any symptoms okay call me bye…"

Was this transcription useful or not useful

CHAPTER SIX: AARON

This was the life, Aaron thought as he slid down into the hot tub. Jackie was out of town, the kids were at camp, and he had this glorious evening to enjoy a bottle of Don Julio and a neon sunset. Dan Fogelberg sang his mellow tunes of heartache and woe on the outdoor speakers; the only other sounds were the birds chirping at the setting sun, the rattle of leaves in the woods, and the gurgle of the water jets.

He'd been feeling horny all day, his hands down his pants half the time he worked on his web sites, arousing himself as he conquered sales for his company. Each new uptick in his ROI gave him an extra thrust of adrenaline, a tingle in his taint. It didn't hurt that his new product line brought him face-to-face with images of hot men and women in various stages of undress. He was happy he'd diversified when he did, taking advantage of the cheap Chinese trade. Who knew crappy underwear and bathing suits would prove to be so lucrative? God bless Amazon!

He couldn't help but enjoy the water tickling across his nether bits as he sipped and sighed in the jacuzzi. He loved stretching his legs out toward the jets, enjoying the pulse of hot water against the soles and arches of his feet. Every now and then he'd play a little game, lifting his butt off the seat just to see the tip of his penis bob up and down out of the water. The sheer act of submersing himself in water made him feel like a kid again. A horny kid at that.

He rolled the tequila around in his tumbler, the single large ice block clinking against the glass. He savored the heat of the liquor coating his throat, igniting a nice buzz in his brain. He set the glass down, closed his eyes, allowing himself to float up in the water. Another pleasure of being alone: stretching all 6 foot two inches of himself out from end-to-end through the expanse of the tub. Sure, group scenes were fine, but nothing beat having the whole warm world to himself.

As Fogelberg sang about the leader of the band, Aaron breathed in deeply, feeling himself rise with each long inhale, sink with each exhale. Before he knew it the leader of the band was gone and he was in Heart Hotel.

A car door slammed, and Aaron's reverie vanished with an electric jolt. Who the hell would show up unannounced at this hour? Eyeing his towel and clothes draped over a chair several yards away, he calculated how he could get to them without being seen. Figuring it wasn't worth the hassle, he decided he'd ignore the car door, maybe it was a neighbor. Sound carried on nights like this. He took another sip of tequila and waited for the doorbell. But it never rang. He relaxed back down into the tub, floating in his own little oasis, safe in his backyard seclusion.

"Aaron?"

Aaron recoiled, slipped on the fiberglass floor, and plunged into the tub. Gulping in the chlorinated water, he shot up, gasping.

"I didn't mean to scare you!"

The voice sounded familiar. He flung his thick dark hair back and wiped the water out of his eyes.

Oh.

"Daniel."

"Hey. Sorry I snuck up on you. No one answered when I knocked."

Regaining his breath, he looked Daniel up and down head to toe. The thing about these young guys is they could just throw any cheap H&M shit on and still look good, while the rest of Connecticut grown-ups were drowning in Vinyard Vines and Brooks Brothers.

"Hand me my towel, would you?" Despite the fact that he'd been naked any number of times with Daniel, he was not about to flash him now.

"Don't get out on my account." Daniel wandered over to the tub; Aaron reflexively covered his crotch. Seeing this, Daniel smiled. "I'm not going to bite."

"I don't know if I can be sure of that," Aaron said, unable to conceal a smile.

Daniel turned away, lost in the quiet of the woods, the last act of the sunset broadcasting itself orange, red, and lavender across the lenticular clouds on the horizon. "I miss nature. I miss sunsets."

Happy that he'd thought to bring the bottle of tequila with him, Aaron swirled the remnants of his drink in the glass and downed it all at once.

"Ah, Don Julio. Special night?" Daniel turned back to face Aaron.

"Just enjoying a night alone."

"Jackie's in D.C." Daniel nodded.

Aaron looked up, alarmed, how did Daniel know that? Were they being stalked?

Seeing Aaron's reaction, Daniel put his hand on the edge of the tub. "I saw it on her Facebook feed."

"Oh. I thought she blocked you. " Aaron settled back down. "So, what can I do you for?"

"I'm working up my 12 steps," Daniel said, his voice low, chin dipped. "You know, making amends, all that. Jackie tell you I stopped by the other day?"

"She did not." He poured himself another healthy shot of tequila. "I didn't bring out two glasses. Want a sip of mine?"

"Naahh," Daniel said, kicking at something on the slate pad. "Okay. Maybe."

Aaron handed him the glass and watched as Daniel took at first a small sip, then downed the rest in one gulp. For a moment he looked as if he were fortifying himself against something.

"Finish it up, why don't you?"

"I'm sorry, it was involuntary." Daniel held out the glass, the lone block of ice quickly shriveling.

"S'okay," Aaron said as he took the glass and poured himself some more. "Listen, I don't get involved in *d'affaires des mes amis*. Especially the gays. I don't understand all of..." he paused, swirled the drink, and downed it. "Whatever it is you guys do."

"It's no different than what you guys do, what you fantasize about, really, although we're more likely to put it into action, I guess – can I jump in?" He was looking at the tub like a kid watching his friend eat a popsicle.

Maybe it was the tequila talking, Aaron wasn't sure, but for whatever reason, it seemed reasonable. "Sure, why not."

It took only seconds for Daniel to kick off his flip-flops and jump out of his shorts and t-shirt. He climbed up the stairs and stuck a toe in. From his vantage point below, Aaron couldn't help but take in the giant hose dangling between Daniel's legs. He'd seen it before of course, heard legends about it, but now, seeing it from below, he felt as if he were looking up at a Macy's balloon of a hot dog. Okay, it *was* the tequila.

"Ouch!" Daniel exclaimed as he sucked in his breath and stepped down into the tub, the water just to his shins.

"You gotta take the plunge, buddy," Aaron said, averting his eyes, pretending to be absorbed by the sunset.

Daniel let out a series of oofs, oohs, and aahhs as he stepped lower into the tub. "I feel like a lobster being led to his death."

"But what a way to go!" Remembering he'd come prepared, Aaron turned around and fished for something near the cup holder. He pulled up a round white cylinder and displayed with glee. "It's medicinal!" He took a long pull on the pen and let out a slow stream of vapor, which twirled away with the rising mist of the tub. He extended it to Daniel.

"Well hello d'ere!" Daniel said in his best cartoon voice. Holding the pen like James Dean, he took a long drag and blew the vapor up into the air.

Aaron, feeling the fast effects of the cannabis, relaxed with a pronounced sigh. At this point, he really didn't care who was in the tub with him. It all felt like people soup now, warm and just right for any meal.

"I was just wondering if you could talk to Richard and Seth for me."

"Stop." Aaron held up a hand. "I'm not going to get into it. Whatever happened with you guys, it's up to you. I don't do well with cat fights."

"I think it was more like a dog apocalypse. No survivors." Daniel dunked himself under the water, swishing his sandy hair this way and that, before shooting up again, exposing his ripped abs and the happy trail below. "This feels great, thank you." He scooted back down in the water.

"Don't mention it." Aaron closed his eyes and took another hit off the pen. "I mean really, don't mention it to Jackie. I don't think she'd appreciate me fraternizing with the enemy."

This made Daniel laugh. "I wouldn't call this fraternizing, and I know from fraternizing." He thrust a foot out in Aaron's direction.

Without thinking, Aaron grabbed the extended foot with both hands and twisted, Daniel, with slapstick timing, performed a perfect spin, tumbling over in a wave of water; Aaron was careful to cup the pen in the palm of his hand. Didn't want to lose that, did he?

Daniel jumped up, wiped the water out of his eyes. "Oh, a wise guy!" Again, Bugs Bunny or some such. With a quick grab, he pulled on Aaron's feet until he went under. Miraculously, the pen flew up out of his hand, onto the grass beyond the tub.

Aaron, tipsy from the indica and booze, floundered in the tub, splashing around dramatically. "Help! I'm drowning! Help!"

He went under, came up and gasped, then plunged under again, his right hand shooting up, counting down the time on his fingers three...two...one. When at last there were no fingers to count, he slowly pulled his fist into the water and disappeared with one last burble.

Daniel laughed and began to applaud the pantomime. But Aaron didn't come back up right away. The jets in the tub ceased, and the quiet of the evening became deafening. Daniel waited.

Maybe this wasn't a joke.

Panicked, he dove under, grabbed Aaron from the armpits and pulled him up. Now face-to-face, Aaron spit a long stream of water right into Daniel's liquid blue eyes, and convulsed laughter.

"I got you good!"

Daniel wiped the water out of his eyes. "Why I oughta..." They stood face-to-face in the center of the tub, their chests rising and falling together as they regained their breath.

"You oughta what?" Aaron said, aware of how close he now stood to Daniel.

Daniel didn't answer, just looked up with those eyes. Aaron stood transfixed. He'd thought of moments like this before, fantasized for Jackie on date nights, telling her how he'd put on a show with another guy if she wanted. He swore he had no homosexual tendencies, he was all about the girls, but something about Daniel, his sweet young face, that devilish smile, the inviting eyes. He couldn't help but feel himself stir, and, because they stood so close, couldn't help but feel Daniel's arising curiosity.

"You oughta what?" Daniel asked again, this time his voice soft breathy.

Aaron opened his mouth, but didn't have any words to fill it.

Daniel took the open mouth as an invitation and pressed his against Aaron, swirling his tongue around inside.

Aaron surprised himself by reaching back and grabbing Daniel by the ass, pulling him forward. The sensations were familiar and foreign at the same time: the whiskers around the soft lips, the erection pushing against his thigh, the muscular round cheek, so different from a woman's but so…inviting. He felt Daniel's hands on his own ass, as they pressed together from head to crotch. Aaron grabbed Daniel by the shoulders and pushed him away.

"What are you doing?" he asked, now gulping for air.

"What am I doing?" Daniel asked, his breath heavy. "What are you doing?"

Aaron felt himself rocking on his feet. Maybe he should have taken it easy on the Don Julio. Maybe he should get out and get some water. "It must be the tequila."

"I was so drunk last night…"

"And the pot."

"I don't remember a thing…"

The vast night sky above spun them around in their own galaxy. Aaron was swaying, ready to fall over like a tree. He grabbed Daniel to steady himself. "Careful," he said, taking a long, deep breath. "I might drown."

"I'll save you."

Aaron grabbed Daniel by the back of the head and attacked him like a priest on an altar boy. He had no idea what he was going to do, but now was the time to do it.

* * *

"You can just let me out here," Jackie said to the Uber driver. Happy that her seminar was canceled at the last minute (she still kept her deposit!), she was happier to have the night alone with Aaron. What a perfect surprise!

The driver opened the trunk and handed her the suitcase. "Sure you don't need help with this?"

"No thanks, I'm good." She reached into her bag and grabbed a ten. "Here — I'd rather give you the cash. I'll rate you five."

She waved as he drove off. Opening the mailbox, she was surprised to find it empty. Aaron never picked up the mail. She shook her head in surprise. *Will wonders never cease?*

She was about to find out they never did.

Voicemail

Unknown caller
Mobile

Transcription Beta (low confidence)

"Oh Aaron you must be punished everyone will know soon enough everyone
"

Was this transcription useful or not useful

Book Three:
The Dick of Daniel

CHAPTER SEVEN: RICHARD AND SETH TAKE WALK IN THE WOODS

Seth pulled a large backpack out of the back of the Range Rover and hoisted it over his shoulders.

"You don't have a pup tent in that thing, do you?" Richard asked, eyeing the over-sized canvas bag with all manner of zippers and geegaws. "Are you smuggling small Jews into Connecticut?"

Seth rubbed Richard's head affectionately. "Very funny. More like smuggling bagels and lox for the deli-starved WASPs."

Richard gave Seth the side-eye. "You're not planning on camping, are you? Because my idea of camping—"

"Comes with a feather boa, I know." Seth loved finished Richard's well-honed jokes.

"Don't think I'm going to carry that thing."

"I wouldn't dare. Anyway, I need the exercise. Your baking has made me gain a few pounds."

"Best anti-depressant in the world." Richard surveyed the area, taking note of the name once again. "You're sure you just don't like this park for the name…Cockaponset?"

"Wait a minute wait a minute…" Seth stopped and pondered this. "Cock-a-ponset! Oh no! Like a penis, right? I never would have thought about that. Cockaponset…"

"The old jokes really are the best." Richard shook his head, looked around. "Which trail are we taking? I'm only wearing sneakers."

Seth indicated a blue trail sign up ahead. "The blue trails are for foot traffic only. I don't want to compete with off-road maniacs."

"You and me both." Richard put his hand on Seth's shoulder and before long they had disappeared into one of Connecticut's biggest state forests. Like most of Connecticut, its landscape was formed during the ice age, when retreating glaciers gouged the Appalachian mountains, leaving boulders and rock formations behind. What made farming a pain in the ass, made hiking a real pleasure. *If you like that sort of thing.*

Richard only *kind of* liked that sort of thing.

"I don't suppose there's a concession stand along the way," he asked after forty-five minutes of gentle uphill hiking. "Better yet, a saloon with sarsaparilla cocktails."

"Why do you think I brought this huge backpack? I know my husband!"

"Oh goodie! It's five o'clock in Greenland, let's drink."

Seth checked his watch. "Actually, how about another forty-five minutes?" He hiked ahead as Richard dawdled.

"You don't want to sit down? You always want to sit down." Richard was beginning to get an idea that Seth had a hidden agenda. He watched Seth tromp ahead, his broad shoulders swaying. He hurried to catch up. "Why all the mystery?"

"Mystery? Why would there be a mystery?"

Richard stopped. "Well for one thing, you're moving like they're going to feed you dinner at the end. For another: when do you insist I go hiking with you?"

"I just thought you'd like this place."

Richard looked around. "Trees, rocks, birds…" he pointed to some debris. "Abandoned water bottles and potato chip wrappers. Yup I like it."

"Such a city boy." He shrugged the backpack higher up on his shoulders. "Grab a water out of the back here, will you?"

Richard fumbled with a zipper. "Which pocket is it in?" He tried several compartments that looked like they could have contained a water bottle. A bottle of Boy Butter fell out of one of them. "Say, wait a minute…" Richard picked up the bottle of lube as if he were discovering a clue. "Something tells me you've got more than hiking on your mind."

"Give me that." Seth snatched it back. "It's the one that has the bottle in it." He reached around to hand back the lube.

Richard replaced the Boy Butter and fetched a bottle of water, twisted off the cap and took a healthy swig. He held it out for Seth, but pulled it away playfully when Seth reached for it. "Oh, I don't think there's anything for me in that black bag."

Seth grabbed the bottle and downed the remains in one fell swoop.

Richard sat down on a bolder, happy to watch his husband in his favorite environment. Despite Seth's city upbringing, his high-end education, he really was just a work horse, an ox, fit for the outdoors. "You know this park pretty well, don't you? When did you come here?"

"Before we met."

"Don't tell me, the Fresh Air Fund for Brooklyn Jews."

"Har har." Seth checked his watch again. "Come on we've gotta go."

"Gotta go, huh?" Richard crossed his arms. "Not until you fill me in. You keep checking your watch like we've got reservations."

Seth held out his hand for Richard to grab. "Keep walking and I promise to fill you in on the great mystery of Cockaponset."

Richard eyed his hand suspiciously, as if he might pull it away like Lucy with Charlie Brown's football. He squinted a bit, trying to ascertain what his husband was up to, but as always, the dimpled smile and little boy grin were impenetrable. "Okay...but spill."

"The truth..." Seth began, holding Richard's attention dramatically. "Don't get mad."

"This does not sound good."

Seth grabbed Richard by the hand and they walked up the trail, Seth trying to say this in the best way possible, one that wouldn't alarm Richard. One move, like a Band-aid, he thought.

"I used to come here with Daniel." He felt his breath halt a moment. Maybe the backpack was too heavy after all. Or maybe the truth was.

"Daniel..." Richard repeated.

"Only a few times. When you were on deadline and I wanted to get out of your hair."

"Okayyy..."

"He's much more out-doorsy than you, and he knows all of these parks from when he was a kid. His family went camping."

"Go on."

Seth stopped and looked at Richard. "Now you're getting mad. And I haven't said a thing."

Richard stuck his hand in his pocket. "I'm not mad. But something tells me I'm going to be mad."

Seth grabbed Richard's face in both hands, leaned his forehead next to his. "I love you, you know that. You are number one in my life."

Richard pulled away before Seth could kiss him and walked ahead. "So you came up here and fucked Daniel, is that it." He didn't look back as he picked up his pace.

"It's not like that."

Richard swung around. "Oh, it's not like that, is it? Then tell me, what was it like?"

Seth hurried to catch up, the pack weighing him down. "Okay, maybe it is like that. But I didn't think you'd mind. Not really. After all, it wasn't cheating, it was Daniel."

"But you never told me."

"I know, and it was wrong, and I'm sorry, now slow down, will you?" He bent over, hands on knees, gasping for air. "I can't keep up."

"Oh, I thought I wasn't keeping up."

"Don't be that way."

Richard reared. "I *am* that way! I thought that's why you loved me. Because this is *exactly* the way I am."

Seth held up his hand, as if to stop the onslaught. Once Richard got started it was like being put on the stand by Clarence Darrow himself. Every little twist and turn of their lives was put on exhibition, then examined and cross-examined. Seth wasn't in any state to take this, not today. Not like this.

"Stop," Seth gasped. "Please, just stop." He keeled over, his knees crunching in the dirt, the backpack bending him over. His breath came in gasps and wheezes.

Richard turned, saw that Seth wasn't play-acting, and hurried to his side. He grabbed the backpack and pulled it off Seth's shoulders, tossing it to the ground.

Continuing to struggle for breath, Seth tried to go on, but soon sobs were interrupting his speech, a staccato series of unrelated words. "I. Didn't. Sorry. Can't. Just…"

Now feeling guilty for his melodramatic display, Richard knelt next to his husband and stroked his back, bristles of trimmed hair poking through the sweat-soaked t-shirt. "It's okay. It's okay." Now his concern went far beyond their argument. He always forgot that, although Seth was in great health since his surgery, his whole system was compromised. His doctor had recently changed treatment, upping the androgen blockers for the third time. Even though Seth joked that it was all putting him into menopause, the reality was, his body was changing faster than either one of them cared to admit.

Seth leaned against the base of a hickory, slowly finding his breath between gulps and tears.

"I'm sorry," Richard said, stroking Seth's cheek. "I'm sorry. I didn't mean to upset you."

Seth grabbed Richard furiously, pulling him in, as if he were being rescued from drowning. "No. I'm sorry. I'm awful. I didn't mean this to hurt you."

Together they rocked back and forth, exchanging the same string of apologies every devoted couple repeated and recapitulated since the beginning of time. Sleights and indiscretions passed down from mothers and fathers, an ouroborus of insecurity and damage, coalescing in these two men who loved each other despite it all, or perhaps because of it. They were distorted reflections of each other in the weird carnival mirror that was marriage. Now they tried to make it all better with kisses and hugs, epithets of love and affection.

His breathing now under control, Seth unzipped a flap on the backpack and retrieved two protein bars. They sat quietly and ate, listening to the quiet of the forest. Unseen woodland creatures rippled the undergrowth, fluttered in the treetops.

"I made a date for us to meet Daniel," Seth said at long last, neatly folding up the protein bar wrapper. "Up here. A special place. I wanted to surprise you."

Richard sat quietly, chewing on his bar.

"It didn't take a sleuth to see how much you were pining away. Sometimes you and I would be making love, and I knew you were somewhere else, touching some ghost." He reached over and rubbed Richard's knees. "We got so caught up in punishing Daniel, for everything he did, that I think we lost our way. Who, in the end, were we really punishing?"

Richard shut his eyes, tears splashed down his cheeks, but he made not a sound.

"It's not a bad thing, honey. We opened up this chapter in our marriage, and no matter how devastating it was, how it all blew up, there were real feelings. And with real feelings of love, we have to find real forgiveness. For our sake, not just his."

Richard nodded his head, wiped his cheeks.

Seth looked at his watch, glanced up the path.

"Okay," Richard said quietly, hoisting himself up. "I don't promise anything once we get there. But you tell me everything."

And so, as the two made their way up the winding path, Seth told him *just about* everything. About his hikes up mountain paths with Daniel, sojourns in the woods, matinees in tents by streams and lakes. As Richard warmed up to the stories, he began asking specific questions, like "What did you do?" "Did you think you'd get caught?" "All that? In the woods?" "Could anyone see you????"

By the time they neared their destination, Seth had confessed his actions, and his undying love for Richard, as well as the remaining love for Daniel. Perhaps he neglected to tell about a recent trip to Daniel's squalid digs, but really, that was just a frivolous detail, wasn't it?

For his part, Richard allowed himself to play wounded bird in all of this, never indicating that he, in his own way, had been a predator in this convoluted relationship.

Seth spotted the unmarked turnoff —by a triple oak—that led to their special hideaway, a canopy of trees and grape vines, far from the trodden path. He checked his watch. "I think we're a little early." He looked closely at Richard. "You okay?"

Richard took Seth's hand and placed it on the bulge in his pants. "I've had this since you told me the first story about that blowjob up at Sleeping Giant State Park."

Seth laughed, took Richard's hand, and guided him up the meandering path. Exposed roots of oaks and maples acted as steps, footholds to make the climb a little easier. About 500 feet from their destination, Seth held a finger to his lips.

"Shh. Listen."

They stood still, trying to decipher the feint, nondescript sounds. Were they animal or man? Seth carefully dropped his backpack and crept ahead, Richard close on his tail. At last they reached a veil of vines dangling from overhead branches. Seth parted them and stopped still in his tracks.

The world narrowed to a tiny pinpoint of activity, as if he were looking through the wrong end of a telescope.

There, in the center of the clearing, writhed a naked human pyramid. Daniel, riding behind the upturned ass of a young stud, was thrusting away, eyes closed in ecstasy. Behind him, bucking in counter-rhythm, was a muscled, tattooed hunk, hands on Daniel's hips, grunting in pure pleasure.

Daniel opened his eyes and smiled, as if welcoming long lost friends to his party.

"Well hello d'ere," he said in his familiar comical voice. He never stopped his humping and swaying.

Now the boy in front looked up, revealing a shy grin.

"You know Kyle, of course." He slammed extra hard, sending the boy to his elbows with a gasp somewhere between elation and pain. "And...oofff—" he was momentarily interrupted by a particularly violent thrust from behind. "...of course you know Dylan."

The Marine waved at Richard and Seth. "Heya guys."

Seth reeled back, as if he might collapse. Richard caught him, his entire body rigid.

"Come on in!" Daniel said between grunts. "Why don't you join us?"

CHAPTER SEVEN: DANIEL'S DAY

S ome say revenge is a dish best served cold. I prefer to dish it
out *piping hot.*
　　　So Richard and Seth got just what they asked for. Bit by
bit, little by little, I made my way back to them. But this time the
stalking wasn't to ingratiate myself to them, but to make them pay.
After they discovered I'd been selling videos of us all fucking – as
well as nice duo scenes – their retribution was swift and decisive.
Not only did I lose my livelihood as Seth's foreman, I lost my
apartment, any savings I'd scraped together, everything.
　　　So yeah, I fucked 'em good this time.
　　　Listen, I've been used my entire life. I've been a convenience
to everyone I've known. A packhorse for my parents – who to this
day call me only when they need something. Or men? Yeah, it's all
about Big Dan's dick isn't it? They all love me for that one
appendage. Is it my mind they're after? Fuck no. I'm pliable and
convenient for them to love and fuck and keep around like a pet –
another kitten or puppy for them to coo over. And when I do the
slightest fucking thing wrong what do I get? Busted down to
civilian.
　　　Okay, so maybe it wasn't a trivial thing, I get it. But who is
really going to find out? If you're online looking for jerk-off
material of guys on guys, what does that say about you?
"Uhhhh…I'm sorry, Seth, I'd hire you to landscape my seafront
property, but then the wife and I saw you getting barebacked by an

eight inch dick, and well, I don't think you have the morals needed for our arborvitae hedge, nuh-uh."

Shit, right?

Or how about "Yes, Richard, your critical analysis of Faulkner's racism is interesting, but I saw you gulping down a load of man spunk, so we won't be publishing it."

Need I say more? I mean, for Christ's sake, I had to do something for money. Real money. You think Seth paid all that great? Here I am, cuddled and cradled in all this opulence, and then I go home to my shit-hole apartment. When do people like me get to have something? To know true luxury? Porn was my way to prosperity. And people were willing to pay big. And they took it all away.

So I went underground and set traps. You think they'd be able to get a donut whore or a Marine on their own? Seriously? Sure, Richard might be able to sweet talk someone into a fuck using Seth's hairy chest as bait, but when someone could choose my equipment over theirs, what do you think?

So I groomed them. I "interviewed" guys. I auditioned Kyle and Dylan. Of course I didn't let on what I was doing, just led them by the nose, pointing them toward these two hot daddies (you don't like "Daddies" Seth and Richard? Well fuck you! What else do you call old guys who are on the lookout for boy pussy? I mean, call uncle all you want, you are a Dad in a Dad bod. Get the fuck used to it).

Do I feel a little guilt in putting those two sweet boys in danger with them? I mean, how much danger could they be in, with those two Daddy wimps, right? Okay, so Seth and Richard had their own game going on, score one for Richard! When Kyle told me about the whole "discover" scene with Seth in a rage, I smelled bullshit. Richard doesn't do accidents. Everything is plotted and planned down to the letter. He even drove the fucking red Spyder? He never takes that thing out, really (still wondering who he blew to get that one).

I thought maybe I should warn Dylan with his PTSD and all. Seth lays out a pretty good trap, bear hugs and all.

But...

You want to fuck your way to the top? Be prepared to bottom.

Except, all things considered, Seth is really the bottom guy, just using the next big package to sate his bearish, boorish appetite. I know what my appeal is. Sure, they might be all 'we love you' and shit like that but in the end I'm nothing more than a dick.

Not that I'm complaining.

Christ, you know? You get busted down to nothing and you're scrapping your way back from the pits. And that's what gets me. Sure, I put their pictures online, and sure, you could see them fucking their way from here to kingdom cum, but is that really a reason to destroy me? It was my ass and my cock too, you know.

I'm going to lay this all at Richard's feet. Seth doesn't have the wherewithal to mount a prolonged attack. He doesn't know the long game. Seth might have the temper, he might be the ramrod, but Richard is the general up in an air-cooled tent calling the shots. So I went after him too.

You think he's all innocent?

A month or so after the whole shit storm and the legal actions, I did indeed get a job at a bookstore. At *that* bookstore. You know the one I mean. One with adult products in front, dildos, butt plugs, nipple clamps, and booths in back where men can fall to their knees and come to glory.

(That's glory *hole* for you uninitiated: a hole in a wall for people to suck anonymous dick or have their anonymous dick sucked).

So yeah. Turns out Richard keeps up on his apps. And *"2-4ThePrice"* wasn't such an original *nom d'app*, if you get my drift. I'd recognize that overly erudite profile: "likes a man who can hold his own in the bedroom or in the boardroom. Someone who can read Hemingway and read our beads." Okay, I almost puked just typing that last line. Wonder how he doesn't die from insincerity.

(You can't spell sincere without sin!)

And also: you think I wouldn't know Seth's hairy pecs and Richard's upturned…smile…if I saw it in a moonlit alley? The thing is: when you're on a stealth mission, it's pretty easy to infiltrate (just ask Putin) when the subject is gullible. And Richard wasn't too keen, he didn't really notice the new guy stalking him out there in the cyber app world of come-fuck-me-now.

So I draw Richard my way, to the bookstore. With my new Scruff handle (and no I will not divulge) he has no idea it was me.

I keep my equipment in well-manicured shadow in all my pix. Stole a face pic from some turd in Baltimore. I get him hot and bothered, promise him a taste of me if he made his way to the bookstore at such and such an hour. It takes a lot of patience, a lot of coercion, but when I see him coming in, I ask my co-worker to take the cash register. I go into the back and wait (we have surveillance cameras back there, you should know, if you're one of those straight guys lookin' for a little head because your wife can't slurp you down, we got footage and we'll turn it over to the police – or a lawyer – in a heartbeat).

This first time, I'm watching the monitors, and I see Richard (wearing a black hoodie and jeans for criminy sakes, like Cary Grant in "To Catch a Thief") mozying around, looking for two empty 'studios' in the slimy, jizz and Clorox-scented back room. And he finds one! I'm on my mark, but wouldn't you know, the one next to him has a busted out light and there's a fat guy in there, peering through the hole, waiting to be crammed). So I quietly whisper, "sorry we gotta do some repairs here, here's a voucher, please step aside," and I just push him out, belt buckle clinking, him holding up his unzipped pants). I give myself a good grab and come up nice and hard in two tugs and shove my eight inches through.

I admit, feeling that familiar mouth brought me back to happy times, like the backseat of our Camry when I was 15, the steam room at the Seattle Y, or, if you're all smart and shit, like eating a cum-soaked Madeleine.

I resisted the urge to bend down, to peek through that hole, to give Richard the satisfaction of him knowing that I know who is sucking me off, because let's face it, there is only one cock like mine and Richard knows every bump and vein. And he's going it at it like he hadn't had a belly full in months (which, considering Seth's condition, is probably true). I gotta admit, I felt more than just that familiar tingle, the rising flood in my loins, the blowing of Vesuvius. I felt kind of…let's just say I *felt* and leave it at that okay.

So he's going at it and it doesn't take long for me to erupt. He was always the best at the last part, clamping his lips down with the first shot, sucking a little harder with each additional spurt, cupping the balls and tugging to get every last drop and the shudders and the shivers and the grunting.

If it isn't the cock, the grunting is the giveaway. Sucks to have jerked it all those years at my parent's house. I never learned to let loose. I don't sing. I don't wail.

I admit he has me spent. I nearly collapse onto that semen-soaked bench (NEVER sit in those booths – you've been warned), but manage to catch myself and my breath. I'm hoping to get out real quick, but my hands are actually shaking as I try to zip up. That's when I hear it. His soft voice.

"I've missed you."

Well you can imagine the world spiraling out of control as I take that in. I hold myself together, bite back everything that's in my mouth, every errant phrase that pops into my brain and I real quick buckle up (zipper be damned) and I hurry outside. I gotta talk to him. I gotta tell him that he was a fucking shit and how could they do that to me and how could you miss me or was it my dick that you missed and fuck you fuck you fuck you.

But he's gone.

Once again, I go out in front to look out the front window (under the neon XXX sign) to see him high-tailing it out of there. NOT in his Spyder I might add.

And so we become regulars.

He knows what he needs; I knew how to give it to him.

Plus the tips. Did I mention the tips he shoves through that hole like I was some goddamned Holly Golightly whore? Of course I take it. Fuck you Richard.

That's when the whole idea to play poor, poor, pitiful me comes up. I have Richard right where I want him (on his knees sucking on my joint). Now to get Seth. But that's easy. Seth is the fix-it guy; he always wants to be useful. So I play the "I didn't know who else to call," damsel in distress thing – appeal to his soft side. You should see me messing up the apartment (the cat pee in the hall came gratis), open cans of beans, water-too-rusty to drink (he bought it, but that doesn't stop him from soaping up in the shower and noticing that the water is clear as Evian). I know that Seth needs to witness first hand my ruination, my utter spiral into the pits of hell. I don't need to take a shower and get to work. I need him to see me naked.

I see it in his eyes. I see the sad puppy dope blinking at me, a whole hokey montage sequence in his brain of us doing the do in better places than this dump. I know I have him, don't even have to reel him in because he is there flopping on the deck like a love-sick flounder.

The real kicker: "Don't tell Richard," almost makes me laugh the fuck out loud. Richard obviously hasn't been telling Seth about our semi-weekly encounters. Again, it's a testament to youth that I can get off upwards of six days a week (God may have needed rest, not me). I had them going and cumming.

I gotta admit, the Jackie and Aaron thing was my signature moment. I wanted to get her too, that bitch who pretends she knows all the shit. So she's a bigshot therapist, so what? I knew she'd fall for the Sharon Stone "Basic Instinct" scene, catching a glimpse of my prized possession. I watched her salivate.

And Aaron had been eyeing my jewels since way back when. You know straight men want it, don't you? They love cock, they love to watch cock, and in their heart of hearts, they want to feel it in their mouths (and hahaha for Aaron – up his welcoming ass!). I got him, I got her. Just to fuck with them.

So the last step is easy.

Seth and I go for a walk up to Park Cock-a-doodle-doo, where we had our secret place. Since the big break-up, I've gone there and met at least a half dozen guys (some secret, huh? Fags figured it out long ago) for some slap and tickle. But Seth is all crying again, saying he loves me and he'll do anything to fix this. So I tell him the only way to do this is take off your pants, bend over, and take my big one for a while?

When I'm getting close, I work my way up into his sweet spot. And we hatch our plan.

"So why don't…" SLAM "you get Richard…" SLAM… "up here for a little *rendez voulez vous coucher avec tu*" SLAM SLAM SLAM… "and we surprise him with a little…"

BEG FOR IT. BEG FOR IT.

"Please…please Daniel I need it. God how I need it."

SLAM SLAM SLAM

I ride him to the ground and he's spread out like Nicole Kidman under Harvey Weinstein, face down in the dirt, munching on grass and begging begging begging for me to finish.

And then in slow motion, I pull back, almost out, almost out...
"You surprise him with *voulez vous coucher avec trois.*"
Grand finale!

He's on the ground crying, and I got my nut off for the second time that day. (Richard is an early riser).

So, yeah. I get Kyle. I get Dylan. Both of them have been hankering for a bit of me after I gave them a taste. (And yes, having that hot Marine all up inside me is better than any Colt Studios fantasy jerk-off session).

But you should have seen the faces on Richard and Seth when they see the *tableau vivant* we set up for them. Just as planned, 2:25 on the dot (Seth is a stickler for early) they push aside the grapevines... and that's why the word *voila* was invented! They looked like Buffy and Jody coming across Mr. French and Uncle Bill doing reverse cowboy in the broom closet. Richard trips, falls over backwards, Seth's nose flares like he's shooting firecrackers out of his nostrils and he's ready to charge.

But face it, Dylan hates the fucking hell out of them, after that humiliation scene. After he found out it was all just an elaborate game and he was the punchline? So he just holds steady, plowing me. Same thing with Kyle, who actually thought he had something. He looks defiant and takes all of me. And the two pansy-daddies go scurrying down the hill all Loony Tunes crazy and we laugh ourselves until we're covered in spunk and sweat.

And yeah, the three of us nap for a while.

I know what you're thinking. You're thinking I'm a manipulative shit. That I could have gone about this some other fucking way. That I could have reeled them in for something nice.

Well fuck you!

You didn't cry every night for months not because you lost it all, but because you had it all. Because you were this close and you knew you fucked up and you knew you couldn't take it back, and you were made to feel things that you never had to feel before.

I had to make sure nobody put Big Dick Dan in the corner!

That night, back home, my groin and butt still pulsing and shuddering from those boys, and the semi-trucks are loud, the dog upstairs yapping up a storm, and I'm thinking okay. Yeah. I'm glad I did this. I'm glad I let them know what it feels like to feel used like that. The air conditioner is broken, the room is hot, the mattress on the floor is crap and yeah I'm glad. I'm truly glad.

I tell myself this as I undress and get into bed.

I tell myself this until I fall asleep.

Voicemail

Joey BB
Mobile

Transcription Beta (low confidence)

"Hey Richard its Joey ____ baby bear _____ hey sorry we won't be able
to make it tomorrow Chaz is feeling under the weather and Mama has
her knick-knacks in a twist haha um maybe we can take a rain check
or whatever really hate to cancel but um you know I know I'd love to
see you but lets figure something out okay love to Seth…"

Was this transcription useful or not useful

* * *

Voicemail

Unknown caller
Mobile

Transcription Beta (low confidence)

"Well Daniel you've been a naughty boy haven't you well your
punishment will be swift and final you blew it again didn't you
_____speaking hahaha…"

Was this transcription useful or not useful

* * *

Voicemail

Unknown caller
Phone

Transcription Beta (low confidence)

"This is a call for Daniel _____ from the City of New Haven Health
Department Clinic. We have the results of your test and doctor
_____ would like you to come in office hours are Mondays
Wednesdays and Fridays but if you call we can fit you in its important

that you contact us at your soonest thank you this is Jeanine Tesatori my number is 203-946-8181 again its in pair a give that you call right away thanks…"

Was this transcription useful or not useful

ABOUT THE AUTHOR

D. Edward Delmar lives in New York and Connecticut and he knows a lot of people.

www.ingramcontent.com/pod-product-compliance
Lightning Source LLC
Chambersburg PA
CBHW020550130626
46552CB00007B/2835